Blind Faith

Sweetshade, Book One

by Delphia Baisden

BLIND FAITH: Sweetshade, Book One

Copyright © 2019

Blind Faith is a work of fiction. Names, characters, places, and incidents are either the product of the author's imagination or are used fictitiously. Any resemblance to actual persons, living or dead, businesses, companies, events, or locales is entirely coincidental.

Published by Delphia Baisden in the United States of America

Printed in the United States of America

First Edition, 2020

ISBN: 978-1-7320371-8-2 (ebook)

ISBN: 978-1-7320371-2-0 (paperback)

Library of Congress Control Number: 2019911266

Cover Art by selfpubbookcovers.com/BeeJavier

Edited by Keren Reed (kerenreed.com)

Proofread by Judy Zweifel (judysproofreading.com)

For my family in Texas,
with gratitude for their unwavering support and
unconditional love

One

Sonny snapped awake, and not for the first time that night. He sat upright, chest heaving, sweat coating his bare skin. His eyes darted around the room, focusing on the soft glow of the nightlight plugged into the wall beside his bed. *Twenty-six and my nightlight is not only a comfort, but a lifeline.*

He turned, swinging his legs over the side of the bed, his feet touching the floor, and slowly began the practice of grounding.

Five things you can see, he recited in his head. *Nightlight, bedspread, lamp, bedside table, water bottle.*

Four things you can touch. Pillow, blanket, book, cell phone.

Three things you can hear. Fan, furnace, my own breathing.

Two things you can smell. He took a deep breath. *My soap, my sweat.*

One thing you can taste. He picked up the water bottle and took a drink. *Water.*

With each step, his tension began to subside. He knew full well why it worked, and he let it do its job. He sat there, breathing through it, feeling himself inch back to some semblance of relaxation, heavily steeped in tiredness. The nightmares rarely let him get more than a few hours before he'd snap awake again.

The first few weeks home, he'd been on the floor and

under the bed before he remembered where he was. He'd absently reach for his firearm, only to realize it wasn't there. He was home, a long way from the actual setting of his nightmares.

And yet they persisted.

He lowered himself back onto his bed, pulling up the top sheet. He closed his eyes, forced himself to remain still, and waited for sleep to return.

The next morning, he emerged quietly from his room, fully dressed and outwardly ready for the day. He stopped in the bathroom to brush his teeth and comb his short-cropped, dark hair, noting the dark shadows under his blue eyes, evidencing his broken sleep. He sighed, turning off the light.

"Morning, Sonny."

He scarcely looked at his mother, Johanna, as he made his way to the coffeepot. "Morning." Not gruff or clipped, just resigned. He felt her watch him pour a cup, studying him. The feeling of it set his teeth on edge.

"Want me to make you some breakfast?" she offered.

Usually he turned her down, but today he only shrugged. "Okay."

He watched his mother make breakfast, moving about the kitchen as she cooked. The same kitchen, in the same house he and his sisters grew up in. It felt strange, living with her now when he had enough retirement money from the Department of Veterans Affairs to afford a decent apartment for himself. But being with family in a familiar place was recommended to him by the otherwise unhelpful therapist assigned by the VA. Maybe it was better in some ways, yet Sonny couldn't help but feel that by being there now, he was tainting an otherwise happy home and their happy memories.

Johanna brought two plates over to the small farm-style kitchen table and sat across from him.

"I'm really starting to get the hang of these tofu scrambles," she commented brightly. He met her eyes and suddenly wanted to burst into tears. He choked them back, nodding, and she added, "Well, you'll have to tell me if I'm right." And just like that, he'd ruined her cheeriness with only a look.

He took a bite. "It's perfect," he said quietly. They ate in relative silence, Sonny holding on to his composure by sheer force of his increasingly weathered will.

Later that morning, he and Jo met with his sisters, Madison and Leigh, at the local Episcopal church they'd gone to since they were children to attend the Sunday service. He knew his sisters didn't believe like their mother or himself, but they'd insisted on coming along after he'd come home. He couldn't help but wonder if that was his mother's doing or if they did it of their own volition. At first it'd been endearing and sweet, making him feel loved and supported. But now he felt like he was indirectly forcing them to do something they didn't want, out of worry for him.

It's been months, he thought as they sat, in age order, in one of the middle pews. He felt the tears again, threatening as they had at breakfast. He chewed his lip, trying desperately to focus on what the reverend was saying, on his words of faith and encouragement. He felt Maddy reach for his hand, not having realized he was gripping the edge of the seat. He loosened it and let her hold it, feeling her eyes on him.

"I'm fine," he whispered. "Sorry." Out of the corner

of his eye he could see her nodding, although now he could also feel the concerned looks of Leigh and his mother.

"Sonny?" Jo's hand on his shoulder doubled the ache of holding back his emotions.

"I said I'm fine," he bit out. He felt her flinch, dropping her hand from his shoulder, and felt his hatred for himself deepen.

After the service, he wished like hell he'd driven himself. He desperately needed to be alone, to let out the pressure building inside, to let himself cry. The nightmares, the guilt, the rage when anything remotely emotional threatened to make him explode, it was all getting to be too much.

"So, lunch? Should we go out?" Maddy asked.

Sonny felt their eyes before he even looked around, knowing they were assessing him for their own reactions. He tensed, steeling himself. "You guys go without me. I can drive myself home."

"Sweetie…" But he turned for Jo's car, walking as quickly as he could.

"I'll bring her home later," Maddy called after him.

He drove home, lost in thought, wondering what they were saying when he wasn't there.

Not only do you behave like a petulant teenager, but they treat you like one. His hands tightened around the steering wheel.

They're just worried, he countered, trying to focus on the lush green scenery. Spring was coming, but it rarely looked like spring this early in Maryland. It wasn't warm, and though the greenery was coming back, the skies were still mostly gray, heavy with the threat of rain or sleet. He used to love it, relishing the hard-won springs and how everything would slowly begin to regain color and life. Now, the laden skies and lingering chill seeped into him, mixing with his inner murkiness until he was sure he'd suffocate. *Seasonal depression*, his therapist had said. *Add that to the list of things wrong with me now that weren't an issue or even a thought before.* Post-traumatic stress disorder, generalized anxiety disorder, major depressive disorder, seasonal affective disorder. There were other qualifiers and add-ons—*wait, there's more!*—but Sonny couldn't remember them all, and didn't want to.

He pulled up to the house and turned off the car. The same old two-story house he grew up in, bearing the same light-blue paint his father had sworn matched his mother's eyes, eyes Sonny had inherited. He'd never dreamed he'd be back here in his mid-twenties, living with his mother. Not out of financial necessity, but for his mental health and stability.

He climbed out of the car, shut the door behind him, and let himself into the house. He placed the keys on their hook, hung up his jacket, and went to the kitchen. Jo had loaded and started the dishwasher before they left. It was finished now, and Sonny opened it and dutifully put the clean dishes away.

If I can't be pleasant to live with, I can at least be helpful. As much as he loathed feeling sorry for himself, he couldn't seem to turn it off. *You're an asshole to your mother, and you can't even paste on a smile long enough to have lunch with your sisters, who tolerate church every Sunday for you.* He stopped, leaning over the kitchen sink, willing away the scathing thoughts, when the furnace kicked on.

In an instant he whirled around, dropping into a crouch, the plate in his hand shattering against the floor.

He didn't entirely lapse into a flashback, but it was a few seconds before he fully realized he was crouching in his mother's kitchen, in the Maryland countryside, in the good old US of A, and that it was just the old furnace that had startled him. He looked down at the shards of glass littering the floor, thankful it was only one of the plain white dinner plates and not one of his mother's beloved Old Country Roses plates.

"Fucking idiot," he muttered, not in anger, but in anguish. He slumped back against the sink counter, covering his face with his hands. And finally, he let go, as loudly and as messily as he wanted.

"Sonny?" And suddenly Jo was there with him. He jumped, immediately shaping back up, wiping his eyes quickly. When had she come in? How much had she seen or heard?

"Shit, you scared me," he said.

"Sweetie, what happened?"

"Nothing. Just dropped a plate," he said, getting the blue-and-white broom-and-dustpan set from the pantry.

"Sonny, you're crying."

"I'm fine. I just thought it was one of your good plates, is all. It wasn't, though, don't worry," he said, trying to shake off her concern. "Don't come in here until I clean this up." Again, he could feel her eyes on him, watching, weighing what she'd seen against what he'd said.

He swept carefully, more because his hands were still shaking than anything else. He gathered the glass with the little broom, pushed it into the pan, and threw it away. She stepped into the kitchen then, coming to him at once.

"Harrison, sweetheart—"

"Here we go."

"You were sitting on the floor, sobbing," she said, this time with an edge.

"Mom..."

"Sweetie, talk to me."

"And say what?" He put the broom and pan away.

"All right, fair, you don't have to tell me about it. But what about that doctor? He's supposed to be helping you with this."

He laughed wryly, shaking his head. "They don't care, Mom." He felt the tears threatening to choke him again.

"Then talk to the VA and ask for another doctor. Or go find one not associated with them."

"What, so I have to talk through it all over again with someone else?"

"Sonny, you need help."

He turned and walked away from her.

"Sonny? Sonny!"

But he stormed to his room, pathetic though it felt, and slammed the door behind him.

At first he stood at the door, forehead pressed against the doorframe, once again losing to the tears. She was right, and he didn't hate her for it. Because this? Jumping at normal house noises? These were sounds he'd heard before and had come to find comfort in during his childhood and adolescence; they shouldn't make him hit the floor in fear. One of his sisters reaching over to hold his hand because she could sense him struggling shouldn't set his teeth on edge as he fought his emotions. His mother's concern shouldn't make him defensive and hostile.

He sat on the edge of his bed, looking around his

room, trying once more to ground himself in the present and find happiness and solace in his home. This grounding wasn't just about finding things to match his senses. This was about calling upon memories assigned to each object he could see. His record collection, some having belonged to his father, some his own. He remembered asking his dad if they still made vinyl records. Sully Lakes's eyes had lit up, and it wasn't even forty-eight hours before his father found a vinyl record store, took his son there, and bought him his first record. It had been one of Queen's live albums. Sonny remembered the twinge of disappointment, missing the crisp sound of a studio recording, but playing it to death all the same.

He stood up and went over to his albums, neatly lined up next to his turntable. He took the old Queen album from its sleeve and placed it in the player. The comforting, nostalgic sounds of rock-and-roll permeating his room, and he felt himself relax a little, the air completely filling his lungs for the first time in…days? Weeks?

He sat down in his old desk chair, closer to the record player than his bed. He leaned back, closed his eyes, and let the music lull him, first into relaxation, then into a light sleep.

Someone was touching him, grabbing his shoulder. He'd fallen asleep, and someone was shaking him awake. Was he in trouble? Was it a commanding officer? Was someone hurt? Had he tried to help someone and passed out, overwhelmed and overcome? When he opened his eyes, would he be confronted with frantic shouts and cries? Had he let someone die again? Images from the past swam in his vision, of blood and organs, pieces of a human body hanging over the side of an infirmary cot, pieces that not only shouldn't anyone see like that, but that there was no repairing and putting back in their rightful place. He flinched at that, jerking away from the hand shaking him.

Jo stumbled backward, landing against his bed, hand covering her mouth.

"Mom!" He was up at once, coming over to her. She tried to stifle it, but he'd seen the fear, the way she'd shrunk away from him at first before correcting herself.

"Damn, Sonny." She was clearly shaken, and trying to regain her composure.

"I am so sorry. I didn't mean to…" He sat down next to her, reaching for her. "Did I hit you? Let me see."

"It was just your elbow. I'm fine."

"Mom." She met his eyes, then let her hand fall. He'd struck her in the mouth with his elbow. The skin was red, but worse, there was a small cut in her bottom lip, and he could see a sliver of blood. "Y-you're bleeding."

She got up and went to the bathroom across the hall from his room. "It's not bad," she said.

He came to her. "Let me clean it."

"It's a tiny cut, Mr. Medic. I think I can handle it." He knew she wasn't afraid of him, yet he couldn't help but feel she didn't want him too close. *And why would she? You just cracked her in the face.* He wrapped his arms around himself. She finished cleaning it and turned, finding him leaning against the doorframe, staring down at the floor. "I'm okay, really. I shouldn't have sneaked up on you like that."

He closed his eyes, tears spilling down his cheeks. "I'm still sorry." He wiped his face with one hand. "You shouldn't have to worry about waking me up."

She shouldn't have to worry at all. He felt it like a lash across his chest.

"You may not want to tell me exactly what happened over there, but I wasn't born yesterday," she said, her hand on his back. He crumbled a little, and she pulled him to her shoulder. The tears came, sobs in tow, though he tried to fight them. "It's okay, baby." She kissed the top of his head.

It's not. He cringed, but she didn't see or sense it. How could she, when he was having a meltdown anyway? He'd never been further from okay.

That night, unsurprisingly, he lay awake. He wasn't sure how he'd ever sleep again after what happened earlier.

I hit my mom. The shock on her face, the fear that lingered at first when he'd tried to get close enough to help her clean the cut on her lip, ate at him, made worse by her comforting him. *I hit her, and she comforted me.*

Normally, he'd toss and turn, anxious for sleep. Not tonight. Tonight he lay there on his back, the covers pulled up to his chest, smooth and uniform in their coverage, his hands folded over his chest. He waited until Jo went to bed, his thoughts cycling from bad to worse.

When he was sure she was asleep, he sat up. He opened the drawer on his bedside table and took out the bottle of sleeping pills his doctor had given him. They acted like sedatives and were supposed to prevent nightmares, but all they did was make him dizzy and make it difficult to get going in the morning.

He opened the bottle, tapped out one pill, then two, then let the whole bottle's worth slide onto the palm of his hand.

You're really going to make your mother find you overdosed on the sedatives that were supposed to help you?

"Isn't it better than hurting her?" he muttered to himself without thinking, then shook his head. He looked at the pills, thirty of them, give or take. It would be enough. He took them, two and three at a time until they were all gone, chasing them with long pulls from his water bottle.

He straightened the folded piece of paper on his bedside table, then lay back down. He covered himself again, lay perfectly still, and waited.

Mom,

I'm so sorry. I loved you and Maddy and Leigh so much more than you all knew. Dad too. I haven't made the mistake of believing I'm going to heaven with him. I'm sorry I couldn't be better. I'm sorry I gave up. If you hate me for it, I understand. Believe me, I hate me too.

I love you, Mom. I know you may not believe that right now. I know you may never forgive me. But I do love you.

I'm sorry.

Sonny

Two

The next thing Sonny knew, he tried opening his eyes and was confronted by an intense brightness. Thinking he'd succeeded in ending his life, tears of relief filled his eyes. When he tried to lift his hands to wipe them, he found he couldn't. He tried again with more force, only to discover that his arms were caught in something. He looked down.

He was lying in a hospital bed, wearing a patient's gown and covered by a plain sheet. His wrists were bound with leather straps to the metal railings on either side of the bed.

"No." His throat ached as he spoke. "No, no no no!" He began to thrash, pulling against the bindings.

"Mr. Lakes!" Someone came through the door, a doctor, judging by her lab coat.

"Let me go!"

"Mr. Lakes, you need to calm down."

"Then let me out of these-these *things*," he said, panicked.

"We can't as long as we deem you a harm to yourself and possibly others."

He lay back against the bed, quivering with anger and frustration. "It was an accident."

"Your mother found your note, and we found a large dose of sedatives in your stomach, which we had to pump to save your life."

He said nothing as tears spilled from his eyes,

running down his temples into his hair.

She pulled some tissues from a box next to the bed and began gently dabbing his tears away. "We want to help you. Unfortunately, right now, this is what helping you looks like."

He remained silent, fighting and losing to the tide of emotion inside him.

"I need to tell your family you're awake. Would you like to see them?"

"No," he said with an involuntary shudder, his voice broken. "I'm sorry. No."

She shook her head. "Don't be sorry. You'd be surprised how common that is."

For the first time, he looked up at her and really saw her. She had a kind if slightly stern face with deep brown eyes and dark-brown skin. Dr. Ford, her name tag read. There was a level of understanding in her tone that caught him off guard.

"T-tell her I love her, though. Please."

"She knows, but I'll still tell her."

Closing his eyes briefly in gratitude, he whispered, "Thank you."

Dr. Ford tossed the tissue in a trash can on her way to the door. "I'll be back soon. Maybe we can talk more and see if we can get you out of that bed?" She smiled before turning to leave.

When he heard the heavy door close, heard the heavier lock turn, he lay back against the bed, turned his face away, and began to cry in earnest.

A few hours and a lot of gut spilling later, Dr. Ford allowed the orderlies to remove the restraints from his wrists. Relieved, he sat up, hunching over his crossed legs.

"Was she upset that I didn't want to see her?"

"May I call you Harrison?"

"Sonny. No one calls me Harrison."

"Sonny. I'm never going to lie to you. I never want to mislead you or sugarcoat anything for you. I don't believe that kind of care would serve you."

"She was, wasn't she?"

"She's your mother. None of this is easy. Not for you and not for her or your sisters. She was hurt, yes. But she has your sisters to support her while you get better."

He nodded, swallowing hard. "I'm so stupid," he said, picking at the edge of the sheet in front of him.

"You're not stupid. You feel stupid."

"No, I am stupid. I made it back home. My mom and my sisters, they're there for me. I got everything back that I had before. And I still… I wanted…" He shook his head.

"It doesn't make you stupid. It makes you human."

He laughed wryly. "It makes me weak."

"I read your file. You're anything but weak."

"Strong people don't try to take the coward's way out, Dr. Ford."

"Sonny, look at me."

He looked up, and piercing dark eyes looked back at him.

"You're only what you think you are. You thought you were weak, and you did what you thought a weak person does. Not that I agree with you, but you're not the first soldier I've ever had in here for the exact same reason and with a similar background."

"I know. I, I wasn't getting much help from the VA. The doctor they had me seeing didn't seem to get it. He tried, but I don't think he understood how bad I felt. Well, feel. So I started researching on my own, looking stuff up on the Internet."

"I don't condone self-diagnosis or self-doctoring, but it's good you were open to other avenues of help."

"Yeah, but it was like falling down a rabbit hole. And some guys, they had it worse than me…" He shivered.

"It can be triggering, hearing things so close to your own trauma."

He nodded. "Very."

She studied him in the pause that followed. "Sonny, do you want help? Do you want to get better?"

He looked up at her again. "I think so. I mean, I did. But then I…you know, gave up."

"So?"

He shrugged. "So doesn't that put me at the bottom of the barrel?"

She frowned.

"Or at the back of the line or whatever?"

"Just because you attempted suicide doesn't mean you don't deserve to get better."

He looked back down at the sheet, thinking it over.

"Don't you think you deserve to get better? To be helped?"

He swallowed hard at the lump in his throat her questions seemed to create.

"You don't, do you?"

He closed his eyes, shaking his head once.

"Well, that's okay for now. Because I promise you, you do."

A couple of days and a whole lot more talking and tears later, Dr. Ford released him into the care of his family. Reluctant though he was, given how little he'd wanted to see his mother and sisters during the psych hold and evaluation, he was happy to be leaving the treatment facility. Dressed and ready, he waited for Dr. Ford to come get him.

She knocked on the doorframe of the open door. "Ready, Sonny?"

"I am." Better than he'd been the night he'd tried to take his life, but still a long way from feeling normal.

She seemed to sense his apprehensiveness. "It'll be okay. Remember what we discussed."

"Almost anything can be fixed."

She smiled. "That's right. Come on, let's get you out of here."

He rose and followed her out to the lobby. Jo and Maddy sat watching for him. Sonny steeled himself, thinking his mother would be angry, would burst into tears. He wouldn't have blamed her for it.

When she saw him, she stood up, and he braced for her to smother him in a fierce hug. But she seemed to pump the brakes, seemed to force herself to approach him slowly. That broke his heart even more.

"I—" He looked away, avoiding her eyes. "I'm so sorry."

Jo closed the distance between them and touched his shoulder, when it was clear she wanted to hug him. "Don't be sorry," she said, her voice rough with the obvious tears she was holding back.

"We're just glad you're okay," Maddy chimed in.

I'm not, he thought, even though he knew from his short time under Dr. Ford's care that that kind of thinking was not helpful. *I am*, he corrected himself. *Even if only for their sakes.*

Dr. Ford said, "Sonny, I have you scheduled for next

Monday with me, okay?"

He nodded. "Monday. I'll be here."

"Mrs. Lakes, Ms. Lakes," she said, and left them.

"Ready to go home?" Maddy asked him.

"Yes, please."

Jo and Maddy had driven in together, and Sonny quickly realized that for the last part of the drive, it would just be Jo and himself. The weight of that hung heavy over his shoulders.

They stopped at Maddy's apartment complex and dropped her off. She climbed out of the car and came up to the passenger side where Sonny sat. He moved to roll down the window, and she frowned.

"Open the door, *ding-dong*." Her voice muffled through the glass, her hands on her hips, she made him smile. He unbuckled himself, opened the door, and stepped out.

"Okay, okay, sorry," he said sheepishly.

"I won't say you should be, but..." She trailed off, her brown eyes sparkling with her usual sass. "You fuckin' should be." She pulled him into a hug. "Please don't do that again."

He wrapped his arms around her. "I promise."

"I love you, you jerk. Call me. Or text. Or, you know, stop by!" she ribbed him. "Anytime."

He squeezed her tight before stepping back. "I will."

She arched an eyebrow at him.

"I promise."

"Okay."

He motioned discreetly at the car and their mother. "Any advice?"

"Just be gentle."

He nodded, and she turned back and walked the rest of the way up to her apartment.

He climbed back into the car and shut the door behind him.

Jo asked, "Do you need anything before we head home?"

"I don't think so. Unless you'd like a coffee or something." She kept her eyes forward, pursing her lips. He added, "My treat?"

"Don't." She put the car in gear and drove them straight home.

The silence between them was thick and heavy, and he could sense her anger building.

She pulled up to their house and put the car in park. "Mom..."

"Sonny, I don't think this is a good time."

He cringed.

She turned to him. "How could you do that? Do you know how I found you?"

"I'm sorry, really, really sorry."

"You looked like a corpse, and you wouldn't wake up, no matter what I did. Your lips were blue, and I really thought..." She trailed off, looking away from him.

"Mom, I'm sorry, all right? I'm not well. I know you know that, and I'm sorry that's how I tried to fix it."

She shook her head. "Fix it? You think that's fixing it?"

"I know I was wrong. I know that now."

"Oh, thank goodness you know now! After you already scared me and your sisters half to death!"

"I am sorry. There's nothing else I can say or do. I can't take it back. All I can do is try to get better and put it behind me."

She sat in her seat, quiet, then said, "Why wouldn't you see me? Why wouldn't you let me help you in the first place? Why wouldn't you talk to me, tell me you were struggling?"

"I, I don't know. I guess it's just—it's a lot, Mom. A lot. I saw things and did things I'm not proud of, and now I'm sick."

"So you turn away? Shut me and your sisters out completely?"

"I don't know how to talk about it."

"You talked to that doctor! Obviously, or she'd have never let you go!"

"I understand how that hurt, I know. But she just, she knew how to get me talking. She's dealt with people like me before—"

"You're my son!"

"I know I have a lot of apologizing to do, and I know we aren't going to see eye to eye overnight. But I love you, Mom. And I am sincerely sorry for all of it."

But she didn't soften. Instead, she climbed out of the car, then slammed both the car door and the house door behind her.

The weekend was tense, things improving between them slowly. Coming back to his room had been difficult, looking around the place where he'd attempted suicide. The only thing that saved him was knowing it wasn't the place that had done it to him. This was still his home, his—if slightly juvenile—sanctuary.

His sisters visited throughout the weekend, and he apologized to both of them numerous times. Leigh took the softest stance with him, and contrariwise, it was the fear and hurt in her eyes that struck him the hardest. At just twenty years old, she was the youngest. And until now, he had no idea how much she looked up to him. He just assumed the girls stuck together and that he was the odd sibling out.

"Sonny?" She'd shown up out of the blue Saturday night after another tense dinner with his mother. He was weary and a bit on edge, startling when she appeared in his bedroom doorway.

"Hey, come in," he said.

She hesitated, looking at his bed. Though it'd been changed and made since that night, she still looked apprehensive just seeing it.

"Actually, wanna go to another room?"

"No, it's fine," she said.

He admired her courage as she came in and leaned awkwardly against the dresser.

"How are you, Sonny?"

"I'm okay. Not great, but not as bad as I was."

"Did they give you any drugs or anything?"

"Nothing fun, I can promise you that."

She snapped her fingers in mock disappointment. "Damn." She sat down next to him, digging a folded piece of paper from her back pocket. She handed it to him. "Don't read it right now."

"What is it?"

"Just a letter from me." She hesitated. "For like, if there's a next time." She looked up at him, eyes wide. "Not-not that I think there's going to be, you know, a next time. But just in case there is. They say it's hard to reach out when you're in that headspace. So maybe not having to, but still having some kind of support, maybe that would help."

He took the letter, felt her messy scrawl through the

notebook paper. How could one sheet of paper, a single-page letter he hadn't even read, mean so much?

"I'm sorry, Leigh." He looked at her, realizing maybe for the first time how young she was and how much he'd forced her to grow up in the short span of a few days.

"Don't be sorry to me. *I'm* sorry. We just, we didn't know what to do, Sonny."

He nodded. "I know. I know it's stupid to say, but neither did I." He watched her face work against the tears welling in her eyes.

"We should've known. Maybe not Mom, but Maddy and me at least. We knew you weren't getting better, and we just kept waiting." She shook her head, catching the first tear with her shoulder.

He wrapped an arm around her, then both arms, hugging his baby sister. "It's not your fault. Or Maddy's. Or Mom's. I, I didn't do it to get away from you guys." He pulled back, looking at her, eye to eye. "You know that, right?"

She nodded. "I know."

"But I'm seeing this new doctor now, Dr. Ford. She's really great at getting me to talk, and I think it'll help."

She nodded again. "I hope so."

"I promise, Leigh. There's not going to be a next time."

She started crying in earnest then, and he pulled her into the kind of bear hug only shared by siblings at the darkest of times.

* * *

"Good morning, Sonny." Dr. Ford came into the room. The receptionist had taken him into her office to wait.

He'd had long enough to drink the Styrofoam cup of industrial coffee and read the diplomas on her wall before she came in.

"Good morning."

She took a legal pad from her desk and sat in the chair across from him. "How was your weekend?"

He ran a hand through his hair. "Not great. Lots of apologizing."

"Did your sisters visit you?"

"They did."

"How was Mrs. Lakes?"

"Very upset."

"I know it's uncomfortable, but that is a normal reaction to a suicide attempt by a close family member."

He sighed. "I know it is. But, I…I don't see how I can really get better living like this."

"Like what?"

"Walking on eggshells, waiting for something I say to set her off. I know what I did was wrong, but…"

"Sonny, trying to find relief isn't wrong."

"I didn't just try to find relief, Dr. Ford. I tried to end my life. And she, she found me. Because I'm living with her."

She seemed to think on that for a beat. "Have you considered other living arrangements?"

Surprised, he looked up at her. "I don't know if that's such a good idea either. I haven't been back six months, and given what I just tried to do to myself…"

"Do you think you're capable of taking care of yourself?"

He nodded.

"Have you been taking your medication?"

"Of course."

"And you plan on continuing treatment, either with me or another therapist?"

"Absolutely. I, I don't want to feel this way. And I don't want to ever feel worse again, if I can help it."

"You seem close with your sisters."

"I am. Maddy, she's like the mom-sibling. Even more so after our dad passed away."

"And Leigh?"

He picked at the fabric of his jeans. "I, I guess I actually didn't know how much she liked me before...you know."

Dr. Ford frowned. "What do you mean?"

"I mean, Leigh's the baby. We're almost six years apart and so different. But she came over on Saturday and gave me this letter." He paused, his jaw working.

"What did it say?"

"I don't know. She told me not to read it unless I got to a bad place again. In case there's a next time, she said." He shook his head. "I think I really scared her too."

"You scared all three of them, Sonny. Your mom's only angry because you scared her. They love you, even if their expressions of love and anger are uncomfortable."

He sighed. "Then why" — he swallowed, steeling himself to speak the truth that'd been growing inside him since the psych hold — "why do I feel like I'm never going to get better under their watch?"

She smiled knowingly. "I think you already know. I think you knew from the moment you told me not to let them back to see you."

He met her eyes. "What do I do?"

"What do you want to do?"

"I think, I think I need to create some distance. Move, maybe."

She nodded. "I think so too."

"But, I mean, doesn't that take me away from my support system?"

"It doesn't have to. I think distance, in addition to continued therapy and medication, would help you heal and regain your confidence much quicker."

He laughed.

"What?"

"Nothing. Just, you know, my mom's going to kill me when I tell her." He laughed again. "I'm a grown man afraid of his mother."

She smiled ruefully. "Not terribly uncommon."

Three

Figuring out where he wanted to go was the easy part. Figuring out how to tell his family? That was what was eating at him so badly.

After his episode, instead of attending church every Sunday, they'd taken to Sunday dinners instead. Rotating houses and preparers each week, they found themselves at Maddy's apartment for this particular meal.

Initially he'd thought of telling Maddy to help him cushion the blow of his news. But then he'd considered Leigh's letter, folded small enough to fit in his wallet, and knew who'd have his back when he announced his plans.

She'd been a little let down at first, but perhaps sensing his happiness when he talked about the place he planned to move to—a small town just outside Corpus Christi, Texas—she'd aligned herself with him.

He'd been watching for her car to arrive, and when it did, he excused himself to "help her carry in" the side dish she'd brought.

"You ready?" she asked, handing him the slow cooker and shutting her car door.

"No."

"Well, the good news is I got this old piece of shit fixed last week. So if we need a getaway car…" She trailed off, shrugging playfully.

"Ha-ha."

"It's gonna be fine, Sonny. Even if they get mad."

"They're definitely going to be mad."

"Hell, I'm mad. But this just means I have somewhere to escape to. Somewhere far enough that Maddy can't keep tabs on everything everyone does."

"Be nice," he chided with a smile.

"Texas?" Maddy asked.

He was thankful they'd eaten first. He wasn't sure he could've done it on an empty stomach.

"East Texas. Corpus Christi. Well, just outside of."

"Is that really a good idea?" Maddy didn't elaborate on the question. None of them did.

"As long as I keep up with therapy, Dr. Ford thinks —"

"I should've known she was the one to plant this idea in your head," his mother remarked bitterly.

He swallowed, shifting with discomfort. "She's helping me, Mom. She thinks the change of scenery, the independence, could really make me better."

"And take you away from your family? Your support system?"

"I'm not going away forever."

"No, I guess not." He heard what she didn't say. *You already tried that and failed.*

"Sonny showed me a couple of houses in that town. Real close to the water, Mom. You'd love it."

"When were you going to tell me?" Maddy asked, taken aback.

"I'm telling you now." He looked around the table at the three of them. His mother, closed off, shaking her head. Maddy, incredulous and annoyed. Leigh, trying her best to spin it happily, trying to smile in the face of what they'd known would be difficult no matter how he approached it. "I'll come visit. And you can always come visit me, especially if I get one of the houses I was looking at."

"How is moving away helping you? Don't you need a support system?" His mother looked at him, desperate and near shaking.

He realized it wasn't anger in her eyes. It was fear. Fear that he'd go off alone, and then who'd be there to check on him? To find him in case he tried to hurt himself again?

"That's what I asked her when I first thought of this. But she said that getting out there, working on being independent, working past the bad stuff, making new friends, maybe that'd be better for me."

"It's clearly not *her* son we're talking about."

He reached across the table for her hand. She tensed but didn't pull away from him. "I know you're scared. I'm scared too. But she says if I stay on the meds, if I keep going to therapy, this might really help me." He watched the tears well in her eyes. "I can't do this—I can't get well—without your support."

"Just at a distance, right?" she spat.

He winced, chewing his lip. "Please, Mom."

She looked at him, and for the first time since his suicide attempt, he caught a glimpse of her as he knew her.

"Please."

She sighed, squeezing his hand. "I don't like it. I really don't. But you're a grown man."

He felt an intense rush of relief at that.

"But you have to promise me—me and your sisters—that you're going to take care of yourself. You're going to stay in therapy and on your medication."

He got up and came around the table to envelop her in an awkward sitting/standing hug.

"I mean it, Harrison."

"I promise."

* * *

Sonny's airplane landed at Corpus Christi International Airport. He'd spoken to the realtor, and with the understanding that he wanted to view his top pick of houses today, the realtor was waiting for him at the airport when he arrived.

Sonny gathered his checked bag, shouldered his carry-on, and proceeded through the airport to where friends and family waited for their loved ones. He surveyed the busy terminal, noting a middle-aged man sitting at a table near a small coffee shop—CO-PILOT COFFEE, the sign read—with two cups perched on the table in front of him. Sonny pulled out his smartphone and called the realtor, Mr. Stephens. The man's phone began to ring, and Sonny approached slowly so as not to startle him.

"Mr. Lakes?"

"I'm here."

He looked up and saw Sonny, recognizing him from the picture he'd sent before setting up this slightly unusual showing. Mr. Stephens hung up the phone, rising with a smile.

"Mr. Lakes." He held out his hand, and Sonny shook with him.

"Mr. Stephens. Call me Sonny."

"Well, then you should probably call me Will."

"Nice to meet you, Will."

"This is for you," Will said, picking up the extra cup on the table and handing it to Sonny. "I was watching the flight progress and figured you could use the pick-me-up. It should still be hot."

Sonny took the cup and sipped through the to-go lid. He took in the bold flavor of the strong, black coffee, appreciating it. "Thanks."

"Shall we proceed to your new home?"

"Possible new home," Sonny corrected as he followed the man out of the airport to his car.

"Of course. Although I think you're really going to like it. And the town."

They drove in Will's car for about half an hour before they passed the welcome sign Sonny had been watching for: WELCOME TO SWEETSHADE, TEXAS.

Sweetshade was a small suburb outside Corpus Christi, and though it was a ways from the coast, Sonny couldn't help but drink up the sunny, summery feel of the place. The usual fast-food chains were right off the main road, along with a few mom-and-pop stores. Tom's Tavern, for one, displaying a prominent HELP WANTED sign out front. He smiled as they passed a medium-sized church—THE EPISCOPAL CHURCH OF EPIPHANY, SWEETSHADE, TEXAS. He'd chosen this town for a few different reasons, and that was one of them. With no family or friends yet, he'd need to find support somewhere, and the church's website looked promising.

They made a couple of turns, drawing away—but not too far—from the business side of town, and started moving into the residential side. For the most part, he saw basic single-family homes. The cars in the driveways weren't the best or flashiest, but they were well kept, as were the yards and houses themselves.

"Here we are." Will pulled the car into the driveway of the house Sonny had been looking at online for weeks, clicking through pictures of the exterior and interior, falling more and more in love with the thought of having his own space.

He climbed out of the car and followed Will inside.

Will took him through every room, explaining about the age and condition of the house. It'd had a new roof installed after the last hurricane season, he explained.

Sonny had to smile. Hurricanes were no joke, but they were also one of the main sticking points his mother had held on to throughout their discussion about where he intended to move.

The house was a simple, somewhat cookie-cutter home. It featured a decently sized kitchen and dining area, a large living room, and a half-bathroom downstairs. Upstairs, there were two bedrooms, both fairly large and each with its own bathroom. The house also had a finished basement with another half-bathroom and laundry hookups. The one-car garage was attached, spacious enough to fit the typical garage junk he'd need in addition to housing a vehicle. The backyard was surrounded by a privacy fence, and a new deck had been added to the back of the house by the previous owners.

Intending to keep it all relatively as it was, he began seeing himself in the house, even clearer than he had while perusing pictures online.

Once Will had worked through his monologue, he turned to Sonny.

Sonny could feel Will watching him, studying this young man with no partner or family as he scoped out a house built for both.

"It's perfect. We're still in agreement over the price?"

"We are," Will said, smiling broadly. "You've made my job incredibly easy, Sonny."

"You've done the same for me. I really appreciate the extra accommodation too."

"Of course! Anything for a fellow veteran. If you're sure, I can take you to your hotel, and then my office will draw up the paperwork this afternoon. Should I pick you up tomorrow morning?"

Sonny nodded. "Absolutely. Only this time, I'll provide the coffee."

Will held out his hand, and Sonny shook it. "You have a deal there, son."

Once Will dropped him off at the hotel—a chain hotel right off the highway—Sonny put down his bags and pulled out his smartphone. He texted his sisters in their group text: *I made it here and saw the house. Probably closing on it this week. Love you all.*

Leigh, of course, was the first to respond: *Yay!! <3*

Followed by Maddy: *That's awesome! Send pics :)*

Maddy had softened a bit since he'd broken the news he was moving, and for that he was grateful.

He then took a deep breath, pulled up his mother's number and called it.

"Sonny?"

"Hey, Mom. I made it. Mr. Stephens took me by the house, and it's really nice." He heard her sigh.

"Well, that's good. I'm glad he was there at the airport. You hear things about those Uber drivers."

He smiled. "I'm careful, Mom."

"I know you are."

The silence that followed was filled with all the tension remaining between them.

"All right, well, I gotta go. I love you."

"I love you too, Sonny."

"Bye."

But she'd already hung up.

Despite his mother's warning about Uber drivers, Sonny called one to take him to Tom's Tavern. Though his VA checks were substantial enough to take care of most of his needs, Dr. Ford had highly recommended that he find a steady job to help create a routine. That, and it would open up the possibility to meet people and make friends.

The Uber pulled up in front of the tavern, and he climbed out. He smoothed down his muted blue and white striped shirt, tucked neatly into his jeans, and proceeded inside.

It was just after lunchtime, and he was hungry. Some trail mix and seltzer water on the plane, and then the coffee from Will, hadn't lasted long.

He took a seat at the bar, even though alcohol was the furthest thing from his mind. The bartender walked over and placed a menu in front of him.

"Hey there," she said. "Day drinking, or just a late lunch?"

"A late lunch, please."

Her green eyes sparkled with humor against her light-brown skin. "Well, that's no fun. But the lunch menu is right here," she said, flipping the menu over. "Personally, the burger is to die for."

"Um, this might be a dumb question, but any vegan options?"

She smiled knowingly. "You'd be surprised. The veggie burger is vegan, and I think the bun is too. No vegan cheese, though, sorry."

"No worries. Plain veggie burger and fries, please."

"Drink?"

"Seltzer water, please."

"Coming right up." She put the order in and promptly brought him his drink. "So, I don't think I recognize you. Visiting? New in town?"

He took a quick sip before answering. "New in town. And actually, I saw the HELP WANTED sign out front."

She crossed her arms playfully, sizing him up. "No offense, but aren't you a little young to want to work in a bar?"

He laughed. "I'm twenty-six."

She looked at him wide-eyed. "You definitely do not look that old, my dude."

"Would you like to see my ID?"

"No, I believe you. Something in the eyes." She motioned to her own eyes, and he felt his happiness slip slightly. She must've seen it because she said, "I'm sorry. I didn't mean anything by that...?"

"Sonny. And it's okay," he said, shrugging it off.

She held out her hand, and for the second time that day, he shook hands with a friendly stranger. "Jean. Jean Landis."

"Harrison Lakes. But I go by Sonny."

"Veggie burger!" the line cook called from the kitchen.

Jean brought him his lunch, and she also placed a form next to his plate, along with a pen. He frowned, looking up at her.

"I like you, Sonny, but that doesn't mean you don't have to fill out an application." She winked, and he laughed nervously. Just as alarm bells began going off in his mind, she laughed. "Relax." She held up her left hand, sporting both an engagement ring and its matching wedding band. "Plus, you're not into women anyway."

He gaped at her. "Th-that obvious?"

"Sweetie, you charm but you don't flirt. At least not with me. I thought I might be wrong, but now..." She smiled, and he chuckled. "I'll leave you to your lunch. And fill out that app. We could use a charmer in this place."

Sonny filled out the application as he ate his lunch. After paying—and tipping—he left the tavern satisfied and happier than when he walked in.

He chose to walk back to the hotel—no more than a mile from the tavern—and get to know the town a little. Tom's Tavern was a standalone restaurant, but not far from the Starbucks/Verizon/Bath & Body Works strip mall. On the other side of the road, there was a grocery store and a small coffee shop. He wondered which coffee shop held the most loyalty in Sweetshade, and couldn't wait to try both. Farther down, he could see the church they'd passed that morning, as well as the post office and a sign pointing toward the town library. He passed the fire station and then the police station, noting how small-town and sleepy each building seemed. Another reason he'd been partial to Sweetshade was that the crime rate was low. Not zero, of course; no place could achieve that. But it was low enough that he could set his mom and sisters at ease.

Once back at the hotel, he checked his email and found that Will had gotten back to him, saying he'd pick him up at nine thirty the next morning and that they'd finalize everything then. Sonny shot back an email confirming the details and meeting time.

Stomach full, mind at ease, he turned on the midday

soap operas, leaned back in one of the chairs in his hotel room, and let himself relax.

It was quiet, almost too quiet. He could feel it, that quiet before all hell broke loose. Any moment now, something would happen. A phone call, a radio call, or, God forbid, a loud BOOM in the distance, followed by sirens. Maybe far enough away that it could remain a distant worry. Maybe close enough that his palms would begin to sweat. He waited and waited in that endless silence, afraid to move, afraid to breathe, afraid that if he did anything, it would set off the horrible chain of events that would come to haunt him.

Suddenly, the phone on the desk began to ring. Only it wasn't the right ring. Not the old-fashioned, tinny ring that would haunt him in the future. No, this ring was softer, less menacing.

And still he froze, staring at the phone, unable to move. Unable to breathe.

Sonny opened his eyes, and for a moment he didn't know where he was. He wasn't back *there*, as his dream had suggested. He wasn't home in his room.

Then it came back to him. Hotel. Sweetshade. New home.

His cell phone—the source of the ringing in his dream—continued to ring, buzzing on the table next to him. He picked it up, not recognizing the number. But with moving and the job application, he decided to pick it up.

"Hello?"

"Hi, is this Harrison Lakes?" A man's voice, middle-aged, but not Will's.

"It is."

"Hi there, this is Tom Shafer at Tom's Tavern. No, the place isn't named after me; that was a coincidence. I hear you're in the market for a job?"

Sonny felt the unease of his dream shift away, like a suspect cloud that never dropped the rain it threatened to. "I am. It's nice to speak with you, Tom. Please call me Sonny."

"Jean said you'd say that. Also said you seem to have the right attitude and charm to work with us. Not sure what that last bit means, but I trust her judgment."

He smiled at that. "She was very kind to me. Am I in for an interview?"

"Well, actually, we do things a little differently here. Sure, I'd like you to come in and talk with me, but I'd like to throw you right in. Some people interview well and can't work for shit. Others interview poorly but shine on the job. I also see here that you're a veteran."

"I am. Army medic, one tour in Afghanistan."

"And you want to work in a bar?"

Sonny chuckled. "I do. I enjoyed some of my time in the service, but the pressure, I..." He trailed off. Most people assumed he'd come back and want to be a doctor or something in the medical field. Hell, he'd hoped he'd feel that way too. Do his duty and then get a full ride through medical school. That had been his original plan.

"I understand, son. Been there, done that."

Sonny perked up. "Oh yeah?"

"Yep! Which is why I'd like to have you come in, meet you, and see how you work. How's tomorrow?"

"Well, I'm new in town, and I have something I need to do tomorrow. Would Thursday be all right?"

"Absolutely. Thursday it is. Ten thirty? We open at eleven, and I'd like to have the formalities and how-do-you-do's out of the way prior to that."

"That sounds great. Dress code?"

"Plain T-shirt, dark for obvious reasons, and jeans are fine. Comfortable but clean shoes. Sound good?"

"It does. Thank you, Tom."

"See you Thursday."

Four

A week and a half later, he was beginning to settle into his new life. The house was his, the job at Tom's Tavern was his, and he'd bought a sensible used truck. His savings had taken a bit of a hit, but working at the tavern and collecting his VA pay would rectify that in no time.

He'd had his things, along with some furniture his mom and sisters had given him, shipped to the house. It was a little thrown-together, but it was a home, a place of his own. When he wasn't working, he was organizing and cleaning the house. It'd been in good condition when he moved in but had sat empty for a few months and needed a thorough once-over. But everything was coming together, and he loved it. No one there with him, watching him, breathing down his neck, asking if he was okay. He knew they meant well, knew his mother cared deeply, but sometimes, even during the bad times, he just needed to be alone.

Once the Internet was set up, he'd emailed Dr. Ford his new information, and shared with her his thoughts and feelings about his current living situation. She'd responded positively and optimistically, which only boosted him further. She'd also passed everything along to a colleague in Corpus Christi, with whom he'd agreed to continue his therapy. He'd been apprehensive at the thought of getting to know and trust someone else after he'd gotten comfortable talking with Dr. Ford.

Nonetheless, he'd agreed and set up his first appointment with the new therapist.

With all that settled, he decided to reach out to the reverend of the church he'd seen when he'd first come to Sweetshade. He sent an inquiry through the contact form on their website and was surprised when he received a phone call in return.

"Hello, is this Mr. Harrison Lakes?"

Sonny frowned, not recognizing the phone number or the voice. "It is. Who's this?"

"Reverend Daniel Charleston. You sent a message through our website."

"Right. I'm sorry. I'm still getting used to the new area code."

"No worries. May I call you Harrison?"

"Sonny, please, Reverend Charleston."

"You can call me Daniel. I take it you're new here. How do you like Sweetshade so far?"

"I really like it. Everyone's been nice, and the weather's much more agreeable. It's been sunny and warm every day since I came here."

Daniel chuckled at that. "Where're you from?"

"Just outside of Baltimore, Maryland."

"I see. Well, we're very blessed with sunshine around here, as you've noticed."

Sonny cringed at the choice of words, wondering if this church would be a good fit for him after all.

"I know it can be intimidating in a new town, being invited to a Sunday morning sermon only to be gawked at by the congregation. Would you like to meet for coffee or lunch first instead? I'd like to get to know you, see if you think the Church of Epiphany would be a good fit for you."

"Sure. That would be great, actually."

"Starbucks or Sweet Bean?"

Sonny thought for a moment. "Unless you're a Starbucks guy, I'd like to try Sweet Bean."

"Absolutely. I try to support local business anyway. How's Saturday morning? Nine thirty?"

"That works for me."

"All right. I look forward to meeting you."

And with that, they concluded the call. Sonny was thankful that Daniel hadn't punctuated it with "Have a blessed day" or anything like that. He was religious, sure, but in a private, quiet way. It wasn't that he was embarrassed; he just felt that grace meant keeping his faith between God and himself.

Saturday morning Sonny was early, more out of personal habit than anything else. He wasn't necessarily nervous, just curious about the reverend. Sweetshade didn't seem too small-town church-y. There were enough chain businesses, not to mention they were so close to Corpus Christi, it would've been hard to truly feel like in a small town. Sonny sipped his coffee—another black coffee like the one Will had waiting for him at the airport. *New place, new me*, he'd reasoned. He'd just relaxed into his chair when a man approached his table.

"Sonny?"

Sonny looked up, startled at first before warming. "Reverend Charleston." He stood, holding out his hand to shake with him.

Daniel arched an eyebrow, and Sonny chuckled.

"Daniel, sorry."

"No worries. I suppose you are young enough to begin with the formality."

Daniel Charleston was younger than Sonny had expected, although he was still likely in his mid-to-late forties. Slightly shorter than Sonny, he was a small, wiry man with dark, thinning hair and hazel eyes.

"Would you like me to order you something?" Sonny asked as he and Daniel sat down.

"No, I actually brought my son along. He's ordering for me and him. I hope you don't mind."

Sonny noticed the young man at the counter, waiting for his order. "Not at all. I don't know too many people here yet, so it's good for me."

The young man brought over a tray with two steaming mugs and a few pastries.

"Sonny Lakes, this is my son, Mason. Mason, Mr. Lakes," Daniel introduced them.

Sonny shook hands with Mason, though he could already sense that Mason wasn't quite as warm and friendly as his father.

"It's nice to meet you, Mason," Sonny said brightly.

"Likewise, Mr. Lakes," he returned.

"You can call me Sonny." But Mason didn't concede or smile at that the way Daniel had, the way everyone had since he'd come to Sweetshade.

"So, Sonny, tell us a little bit about yourself," Daniel prompted, taking a drink of his coffee.

"Well, I'm originally from Maryland. I'm former military. Army. One tour in Afghanistan. But it really wasn't for me, so I retired and decided I needed a change of scenery."

"What was your job in the army?"

Sonny swallowed, working to maintain his composure. "I was a medic."

Daniel studied him. "It's all right, son. I'm not gonna

dig any deeper than that if you don't want to talk about it."

Sonny nodded, a bit unnerved. *He's a father. And a reverend. It's his job to see past the walls. That's why I'm here.*

"What interested you in our church?"

Sonny relaxed a little at the subject shift. "It's the same denomination I was a part of back home. I understand that the Episcopal Church is one of the more open-minded denominations of Christianity."

"In what way?"

He tensed again, not so much at the question, but at the fact that it was Mason who'd asked, not Daniel. "Well, I-I'm gay. The Episcopal Church was one of the first to openly embrace homosexuality instead of continuing to condemn it."

Daniel nodded, seeming to turn that over in his mind. Sonny chanced a look at Mason, who was now pointedly looking anywhere but at him.

"If that's not the case here, then I apologize for wasting your time."

"No, you're correct." Daniel smiled, and as hard as he tried, Sonny couldn't detect anything false in his continued warmth. "I'm sorry, we just don't get too many LGBTQ folks around here. And almost none so forthcoming."

Sonny nodded. "I'm sorry I've caught you off guard. The reverend back home, he was something of a mentor to me growing up, and I just assumed…"

"It's okay. It caught me off guard, yes, but that doesn't mean I think it'd be a bad fit. To be honest, we could certainly do with more diversity around here."

Just then, Mason shoved himself away from the table and stormed out of the coffee shop. Daniel sighed, shaking his head.

"I'm sorry for him."

"I didn't mean to upset him." Sonny dropped his hands from the table, shifting uncomfortably.

"His mother passed away a while back, and for whatever reason, his faith became much more fire-and-brimstone after that. I can assure you, both I and the church I lead are completely fine with all walks."

Sonny nodded.

"Tell you what, you come by tomorrow, attend service. See the place, get a feel for the vibe. If you're uncomfortable, I'm more than happy to recommend a nearby church. And of course, you can always come to me for guidance either way."

Sonny looked at him, still a bit shaken by Mason's reaction to him. "All right, I'll be there. I appreciate it, Daniel."

Daniel drank the rest of his coffee and grabbed two pastries as he rose. He shrugged at Sonny. "Peace offering, you know? See you tomorrow."

"See you then."

Sonny watched him go, wondering if this was his first misstep in his new life. He sighed, looking down at the remaining pastries, knowing there wasn't a chance in hell that any of them were vegan.

The following day, Sonny prepared to attend church for the first time since the move. Dressed in a black button-down, dark-wash jeans, and boots, he'd achieved relaxed without looking too casual. He'd combed his short black hair in the mirror, noting that, though he still looked a bit forlorn, he looked better. Not quite as drawn, his blue eyes not as sullen or bloodshot from any recent tears. *Maybe this place is helping me.*

He had skipped out on his first session with the new therapist. Between the job at the tavern and getting his house in order, it hadn't felt like a priority. Things weren't perfect, but he wasn't drowning like he had been a few weeks ago. He'd get to it, sure, but looking at himself in the mirror, feeling better, he reasoned it could wait while he settled in.

He pulled up to the church to find the parking lot well filled. He was also relieved to see he'd gotten the clothes right. He took a deep breath before climbing out of his truck.

An hour and a half later, apprehension had been replaced by a growing sense of peace. Though a few attendees had gawked at the newcomer, they'd mostly been older and likely just curious. Other than that, he'd been able to slip in and worship like he'd wanted, like he'd been able to do back home.

Daniel had delivered an uplifting, endearingly appropriate sermon welcoming newcomers and people who were different. It might've made Sonny uncomfortable, but the way he'd worded it, distinctly lacking any backhanded words like *accepting* or *tolerance*, gave Sonny hope.

As he headed home, he turned on the radio, which was already tuned to the local rock station, and was delighted to hear the opening chords of the new song by one of his favorite bands, True North. He wasn't one to believe in signs, but he did believe in cues and nudges.

He drove back to his house in a warm bubble of contentment...that immediately burst as he pulled into his driveway and read the word *faggot* spray-painted across his garage door. He sat for a moment, wide-eyed, mouth hanging open, heart pounding so hard, he could feel his pulse in his temples, in his gums.

"No. No no no," he babbled, his hands shaking as he threw the truck into park and stepped out. He walked up to the garage door and studied the paint. Black, wet enough that he was certain it hadn't been there when he left. *No, there's no way I missed that.* He swallowed thickly, pulling out his smartphone. He quickly snapped a few pictures of the garage door before calling the police.

About twenty minutes later, a Sweetshade police cruiser parked on the street in front of his house. A man got out, on the shorter side, stocky, in full uniform.

Sonny had been sitting on the steps leading up to his front porch. Truthfully, it was where he'd landed hard, feeling a panic attack trying to descend on him. He'd practiced the old grounding technique, worked through a few breathing exercises, anything he could think of while he waited.

The officer stopped and looked at the garage door before meeting Sonny on the front walk.

"Mr. Lakes?"

Sonny rose, willing himself to remain calm. "That's me."

"Officer Landis." He extended his hand as Sonny did a double take.

"Landis?"

The officer smiled. "You must be Sonny. Jean's told me about you. All good."

Sonny returned the smile as best he could. "She's been great."

Officer Landis took out a small notepad. "I assume you don't know who did that."

"No."

"Who do you know around here so far?"

Sonny thought for a moment. "Will Stephens, the realtor who sold me the house, although I think he actually lives in Corpus Christi. Tom and Jean at the Tavern. Reverend Charleston and his son, Mason. I mean, I've interacted with quite a few people. But no one's been like…" Sonny shrugged, looking at the garage door.

"I'm going to assume you haven't had enough time to make any enemies around here?"

Sonny shook his head. "I've only been here two weeks."

"And you were able to buy a house?"

"I'm retired army. And I've been saving."

Officer Landis scribbled things down. "Where did you move from?"

"Maryland."

"So it's unlikely someone you might've pissed off there would've followed you here."

Sonny frowned, looking away. "I guess not. But even then, I don't really know anyone like that."

Officer Landis seemed to hear the shift in his tone, seemed to pick up on Sonny's defensiveness. "I'm not blaming you. I'm just trying to get a feel for who you are and who you know." He sighed. "Sorry, Jean is forever telling me I come off like the typical dickhead cop."

Sonny softened a little. "If that were true, you'd have taken an hour to get here and then blamed that kind of vandalism on the queer."

Officer Landis looked up at him then, almost smiling. "Nah, Jean and Abe would never let me get away with anything like that."

"Abe?"

"A friend. Okay, let me take some pictures."

"There's nothing you can do, is there?"

"I'll file a report, but other than that, not really. I'm sorry. It was probably just kids being little jerks and a coincidence..." He trailed off.

Sonny nodded. "Probably."

"It's still good that you called because if this happens again, we can establish a pattern and time frame. So if it does happen again, call us back. Okay?"

"I will. Thank you, Officer Landis."

The officer shook his hand. "Call me Nate."

"Thank you, Nate."

After Nate finished up, Sonny went inside, changed his clothes, and then came back out to begin trying to clean the humiliating word from his new home. As he scrubbed and rinsed, over and over, he thought about it. It certainly didn't feel like a coincidence. He'd only told a few people he was gay, but still. No other houses near him had been hit, only his. And as far as he knew, he was the only openly gay person in town. He wasn't naive enough to think he was the only queer person there, period, but Sweetshade didn't exactly scream gay friendly either.

He'd considered that when he'd decided to move, but in the end, moving hadn't been about finding a partner or a community. It'd been about escaping the watchful eyes of his family and starting over. He didn't want to be alone forever, but as long as he was still learning how to cope with PTSD and depression, he didn't want to see anyone. It didn't seem fair to get close to someone, only to have them find out he was as damaged as he felt. *I hit my mom, for Christ's sake.* He couldn't imagine having a nightmare, his potential partner trying to wake him, and him clocking the guy in the face out of misplaced fright. And then to have to explain when it would just sound like excuses for abuse? He shook his head at the thought.

He scrubbed and rinsed, scrubbed and rinsed, until the word was just a shadow. Still there, still legible, but not the glaring black thing anymore.

He rinsed the suds away and stood back. He'd have to get some white paint and cover the rest of it. He couldn't let his neighbors or, God forbid, their kids see that.

He ran inside and grabbed his wallet and keys, locking up behind him before heading for the nearest hardware store.

Half an hour later, he was relieved to come back and find that, though the shadow of the word was still there, there was no additional vandalism or damage to his house. Grateful, he spent the rest of the afternoon painting over the garage door until you couldn't tell anything, derogatory or otherwise, had ever been there.

* * *

He'd timed it perfectly, and all things considered, he was satisfied with his work. Figuring out which house was Sonny's had been easy, what with the empty moving boxes on the front porch and the SOLD sign still in the yard.

He'd looked around the sleepy street, observing that Sonny's truck was gone as well as many of the cars belonging to his neighbors, and knew he'd been right.

What he hadn't planned on was the black paint staining his fingers. That had been careless, stupid even. He'd walked back home with his hands jammed in his pockets, knowing that if anyone saw him, they'd remember.

At least he'd opted for black. Getting caught literally red-handed wouldn't have been just stupid, it would've been downright laughable.

None of this is funny. *He ground his teeth against his rage, not only at the queer, but at himself for the foolish mistake.*

And still, he made it home and cleaned up before anyone even noticed.

Five

Abe waited for Nate to get back. Hell, he'd stayed after his own shift so he could talk to him. He'd been waiting out by his own car when Nate pulled up in the patrol car.

"I might've guessed you'd still be here," Nate snarked with a smile.

"Larry told me about the call. What happened?"

"You know, we should just make you the honorary hate-crimes unit, Abe," Nate ribbed him, but Abe didn't take the bait.

"Well?"

"Guy's name is Harrison Lakes, goes by Sonny, moved here from Maryland in the past month, works with Jean at the Tavern. But other than her, the realtor who sold him the house, and the good reverend and his son, he doesn't really know anyone yet. Which is strange because someone" — Nate pulled up a picture in the viewfinder of his camera — "spray-painted that across his garage door."

Abe took the camera so he could look closer, flipping his hair out of his eyes.

"You know, if you'd just get a haircut like a normal—"

"He wasn't home when it happened?"

"Said he was in church."

Abe frowned.

"Could've just been a couple of the little shitheads

around here, hazing the new guy."

Abe shook his head. "I don't buy that, and I don't think you do either."

"If it was your house? No, I wouldn't. But this guy doesn't know anyone. He hasn't been here long enough to piss anyone off."

"Maybe someone from back home?"

"I thought of that too, but he's from Maryland. Little far to go to harass someone."

Abe handed him back the camera. "Strange."

"Very. I told him to call us back if anything else happens. But I kinda think it was just a one-off."

Abe wasn't satisfied with that assessment, but he couldn't find another explanation that fit.

"Well?"

Abe looked back at him. "Well what?"

"Aren't you gonna ask me if he's cute?"

Abe rolled his eyes. "That's inappropriate."

"Maybe. But he was."

"Then maybe you should ask him out, Officer Landis."

Nate held his smile, and Abe reluctantly broke into one of his own. Nate said, "He works at the Tavern with Jean."

"You already said that." Abe turned for his car.

"Have a beer for me!"

"Very funny," he called over his shoulder.

As curious as he was, Abe didn't go to the Tavern, vowing to maintain his professionalism. That, and the vandalism nagged at him. Sweetshade was a small Southern town, but he'd lived here his whole life, and no one had ever harassed him for being gay. In fact, he thought people liked having him around as one of their "diversity tokens." He hated that, but he couldn't deny that it had protected him over the years.

So why hadn't it protected Sonny Lakes?

And what the fuck kind of name is Sonny Lakes? Abe wondered as he let himself into his apartment. He'd barely put his keys down before he knew he was going to the Tavern for a beer after all.

"One beer," he muttered to himself, relocking his apartment behind him, and getting back into his car. "One beer, just to see who the fuck we're dealing with." He caught his reflection in the rearview mirror.

Yeah. Sure, Abe.

The drive to Tom's Tavern was quick. He pulled up and looked around at the fairly empty parking lot, spotting one car he didn't recognize.

That's how you know you've lived in the same spot your whole life.

He locked his car, then proceeded into the Tavern.

Sunday evenings were inevitably slow, and Abe often wondered why the small tavern stayed open at all past the church/lunch rush. There were a few regulars inside, mostly older men and the town drunks.

He spotted the new face and nearly stopped in his tracks. *Get it together*, he chided himself, pressing forward. Though Nate had likely said it in jest, he was right. If anything, *cute* had been an understatement.

Abe took the barstool nearest to where the guy was restocking the ice bin.

"Hey there." The guy perked up, a relaxed, handsome smile lighting up his face. "What can I get for you?"

Abe looked at his name tag, even though he already

knew. "Aren't you going to ID me first, Sonny?"

Sonny grinned, but Abe detected a hint of irritation in his bright blue eyes. "May I see some ID?"

Abe reached into his inner jacket pocket and retrieved his badge. Sonny's pretty eyes landed on the glinting gold, and he sobered at once, paling slightly.

"I-I'm sorry, Officer, I didn't—"

"You're new around here?"

Two dashes of color appeared in Sonny's cheeks "I am," he said, rubbing his hands on his short black apron.

Big hands. Abe swallowed, clinging to his charming— if somewhat snarky—self with all his might.

"What can I get for you, Officer...?"

"Ellis. Abel Ellis," he said, holding out his hand. Sonny took it, and sure enough, his hand was warm and slightly damp.

"Abe?"

"Excuse me?"

"It's just, when I spoke with Officer Landis earlier today, he mentioned someone named Abe."

"That's me," he said. "Light beer, please. In a bottle."

Sonny fetched it, bringing it back at once.

"What were you talking to Nate for?" And just like that, a wave of understanding passed over Sonny's features.

"Is that what this is about?"

Abe took a drink, nodded.

"I already told him everything. And I've already washed it off and painted over what was left."

"I don't blame you." Sonny shrugged, though Abe could see the worry in his face, in the set of his shoulders. "Look, I'm not here to interrogate you. He told me about it, and I just wanted to talk to you myself. We don't really get too much of that kind of thing around here." Sonny ran a hand through his short black hair, tousling part of it. Abe had to work to maintain his composure then, taking another drink of his beer and hoping he didn't blush as easily as Sonny had just a moment ago.

"I'm sorry it happened now. I-I haven't even been here a month and —"

"It's not your fault, Sonny." He watched Sonny's jaw work and wondered what he might know and not say. "I just wanted you to know, it's not going into a computer or file and being forgotten about."

Sonny's eyes met his. "Why?"

"Because when something like this happens in my town, I care." Abe held his eyes, and another wave of understanding seemed to dawn on Sonny.

"Oh."

Abe took another drink. "Yeah. Oh."

* * *

Sonny thought of what Nate had said, how Jean and Abe wouldn't let him get away with blaming the vandalism on him. *Jean because she's his wife and a person of color. Abe because they're colleagues and friends and Abe's probably gay.*

"Well, thank you. I appreciate your looking into it," Sonny said.

"How old are you?"

Sonny felt his face grow hot. "Really?"

"What, twenty-one? Twenty-two?"

"Twenty-six."

Abe's look said it all. "You certainly don't look it."

Sonny shook his head.

"I'm sorry."

Sonny looked up at him. "Don't be. Kinda forgot…" He trailed off, not entirely sure how to end the sentence without sounding desperate or lonely.

"How young you look?"

Sonny fought a smile. "Let's go with that." And now it was Abe's turn to blush.

Just then, Jean appeared. "All right, Sonny, I think you're good for the night." She turned to Abe. "I see you've met another of Sweetshade's finest." The sass in her tone was unmistakable.

"Hey, Jean," Abe said, tipping the nearly empty beer to her.

She pursed her lips, rolling her eyes before turning back to Sonny. "You all right to go home by yourself? Want me to stop by when I'm off?"

"No, I'll be okay. It was probably just kids, like Nate said."

"Actually, it probably wasn't. The height of the paint alone suggests someone almost six feet tall," Abe chimed in.

"Teenagers, then," Jean countered. "Would you like to see him home, Officer Ellis?"

"No, seriously, guys, I'll be fine." Sonny took off his apron, folding it and taking his share of tips from Jean.

"Be careful. Text when you get home, okay?"

"Okay."

She flashed a look at Abe before returning to serve the few remaining customers.

Abe slid to his feet. "Sonny."

Sonny came around the bar just as Abe finished scribbling something on the back of a piece of paper. He handed it to Sonny.

"If you need anything, that's my card. My cell

number is on the back."

Sonny met his eyes, startled.

"Anything at all."

* * *

Once back home, Abe couldn't believe what he'd done. He'd just walked in and started flirting with the guy. He hadn't meant to, but the moment he saw him, he couldn't resist. He'd seemed so young and innocent that teasing him had come naturally. And the teasing gave way to flirting.

"I'm such an idiot," he muttered, scrubbing a hand over his face. Closing his eyes, he thought of Sonny's blue eyes, lighter than his own, thought of how he'd only truly looked his age when Abe asked about the vandalism. That was when a solemn, worried look overpowered the youth and warmth that otherwise radiated from the man.

God, Abe, are you really that starved that you're falling all over yourself for the first new gay guy around in ages? But he was, and he knew it. Just like he knew it wasn't because Sonny was gay. It was because, when he smiled, he smiled with his whole face. And when he'd run his hand through his hair, Abe had wanted to do it too, had wanted Sonny to run those big hands through *his* hair.

I'm completely screwed.

* * *

Sonny pulled up to his house. No new graffiti that he could see. He walked around the outside of his house and yard in the growing dusk, finding nothing amiss. He then went inside, locked himself in, and texted Jean as promised.

Made it home. The house is fine. See you tomorrow.

She responded a few minutes later with a smiley face and thumbs-up emojis. He smiled to himself, thankful he had someone who cared this far away from home.

He took the business card from his pocket and entered the numbers and information into his smartphone. *Not that I intend to ever text him or anything,* he assured himself. He plugged his phone into the charger, then proceeded to shower and head for bed.

Monday morning Sonny awoke to a reminder on his phone that he had a therapy session in Corpus Christi that afternoon. He lay in bed, thinking about it. *I'm doing better. Fine, in fact.* Aside from the stress the vandalism had caused, he didn't feel any the worse for wear.

He looked toward the window, the Texas sun already up and beaming into his room. It would be a beautiful day, one he'd much rather spend working around the house and on the yard. He'd bought a new lawn mower, and as mundane as it sounded, he was excited to try it out. He could mow the front and back yards, clean the house, maybe start planning for a small vegetable garden in the back. He didn't have a big yard, but it was enough that he could dedicate one corner to growing his own vegetables.

He sat up in bed and swung his legs over the side.

Yep, that's just what I'll do. And it'll be the best therapy I've had in weeks.

* * *

Abe was greeted that same morning at work by one of

Nate's big, knowing smiles.

"What?"

"He is cute, isn't he?"

Abe shook his head, rolling his eyes.

"Knew it! I'm getting better, right?"

Abe sat down at his desk. "You're getting dumber."

"Aw, come on. Jean told me all about you coming in and flirting with him. Slipped him your number and everything."

"How Jean manages to spy on everyone and still work baffles me."

"So? Are you going to ask him out?"

Abe sat back in his chair, fixing Nate with one of his stares.

"You don't intimidate me, Abe."

"He's a little young for me."

"I always forget you like being the pretty young thing."

"You're such an ass, I swear." Abe laughed. "Anything on what happened yesterday?"

"Nothing. I couldn't even really venture a guess. None of the neighbors I talked to saw anything, or so they say. I don't think it was kids."

"Paint's too high up."

"Exactly. But they had to have done it in broad daylight because he said it wasn't there when he left for church."

"Doesn't make any sense."

"How'd he seem to you?"

Abe met his eyes. "What do you mean?"

"I mean, how'd he seem? Normal?"

"Maybe a little naive, a little young. And talking about what happened seemed to stress him out, but that's

58

understandable. I didn't pick up on anything off. Why?"

Nate motioned him over, and Abe sat beside him, looking at his computer screen. Nate said, "Says here he did a few days in a psych ward back in Maryland."

"What for?"

"Self-harm. Says he tried to commit suicide."

Abe frowned, squinting at the text. "Also says he's former military. Maybe he's got that post-traumatic stress thing."

"Maybe. But it sticks out, you know?"

Abe leaned against the edge of Nate's desk. "What would that have to do with the vandalism?"

Nate rocked back in his chair. "No one saw it. He's new around, so no known enemies. Hell, few known friends. He has a history," he said, looking at the computer screen.

Abe winced. "Kinda doubt he'd do it himself. That kind of slur? Why not just write a swear word or some shit?"

"I don't know. Not inflammatory enough to really get people's attention?"

Abe gave him an incredulous look.

"I'm not saying he did it. I'm just saying it's weird and maybe we should look at it from all angles."

Abe nodded, going back around to his desk. "I get it. But I just don't think he'd do that."

"Because he's cute?"

"Because he panicked when he realized he didn't properly ID someone for alcohol who turned out to be a cop," Abe said. "Does he have a record in Maryland?"

"No," Nate said, looking away. "He doesn't."

Throughout the day, Abe couldn't shake what Nate

had shown him.

There's no way he did that to himself. But how could he know that for sure after only one interaction?

After work, he told himself he wasn't going back to the Tavern, especially not to see Sonny on a social level. He also told himself he wasn't going to get a feel for him on a professional level either.

I'm going to get a beer, he insisted as he found himself behind the wheel of his car for the second time in twenty-four hours, headed for the Tavern.

* * *

Sonny was nearing the end of his Monday night shift when he spotted Abe at the bar. Same blond hair, same smile that probably got him laid as well and as often as he wanted.

Why are you thinking about him getting laid, Sonny boy? He smiled as he approached him.

"Hey," Abe said.

"Can I see some ID, Officer?" Sonny thought for sure the joke would give him the upper hand.

Until Abe winked at him. "Light beer, please."

Sonny felt the flush crawling up the sides of his throat, felt the smile he couldn't quite stifle. "There you are." He placed the bottle in front of Abe and turned to resume his work.

"Hey," Abe said, and Sonny turned back to him. "Are you off soon?"

Sonny nodded. "Why?"

"I was wondering if you'd like to have a beer with me?"

"Is this some kind of interrogation technique?"

"Why? Do you think you deserve to be

interrogated?"

"What?"

"Look, it's not. I just…" He faltered then.

"Real smooth, Officer Ellis," Sonny said, leaning against the bar.

Abe peered up at him through his lashes. "You'll have to forgive me. We don't exactly have a thriving gay community here in Sweetshade. I'm a bit out of practice."

Sonny looked him over and thought he saw Abe blush. "Yeah. Right."

Abe narrowed his eyes. "What?"

"You get just about anything you want, and you know it." He didn't say it with malice or jealousy, only as if it were a fact.

"Not around here, I don't," he muttered, taking a drink of his beer. "So, is that a 'Fuck off, Abe'?"

Sonny practically beamed at the touch of petulance in Abe's tone. "No. I'm off in about twenty minutes."

Abe looked up at him, surprised.

"Just one beer, though. I get a little anxious about the house now." Sonny could feel the worry wash over his face when he said it, but Abe seemed to understand.

"I drove by on my way here," he admitted. "Nothing amiss that I could see from the street."

Sonny held his eyes. "Thank you."

Abe studied him for a moment, and Sonny wondered what it was he sought. Because all he felt was gratitude.

Six

Abe drank down his beer while Sonny finished up, grateful that Jean wasn't hovering nearby. Because the more he talked to and watched Sonny, the less he understood why he was there. Was he getting a feel for Sonny because Nate could be right, or was he getting to know Sonny because he thought he might like him?

He watched Sonny take in the fact that Abe had driven by his house before coming here. If Sonny was guilty, he'd be agitated. But Abe detected no irritation in him. Just cautious gratitude, like he couldn't believe Abe would do that for him. That, and he didn't seem alarmed when Abe showed up at his job for the second night in a row.

Finally, Sonny sat down next to him.

"You fellas want a drink?" Tom himself had taken over.

Sonny shook his head. "Just water for me."

Abe looked over at him, mildly confused.

"Sorry, not really in the mood for a drink."

Abe turned back to Tom. "Two waters, then."

Tom poured them and went back to his work around the bar and dining room.

"Why are you here, really?" When Abe hesitated, Sonny added, "I can feel you watching me."

"Oh yeah?" Abe tried to turn on the charm.

"Yeah. Like, testing me, measuring me." He looked

down at the water cupped between his hands. "Am I in some kind of trouble for what happened?"

"Why would you be in trouble for someone vandalizing your house?"

Sonny shrugged. "I don't know. But it just feels like… Never mind." He shook his head, as if he were physically trying to dismiss the thought from his mind.

It dawned on Abe what had just happened. *He internalized it. He's not guilty, but he still feels like it's his fault.* He cringed, knowing he was the one who planted that thought in his mind. "I'm sorry, Sonny. It wasn't your fault."

"I just don't get it. I literally don't know anyone who would do that. I don't even know people back home who would do that." As soon as he said it, a thought crossed his mind. Something about the way Daniel's son, Mason, had behaved with him. *He's just a kid…*

"Me neither," Abe said. He huffed out a sigh, sitting back on the barstool. "But look, I didn't come here to bring you down."

Sonny looked over at him, some of the curious sparkle returning to his eyes. "No?"

"Nope. I actually came to see if I thought you were cute, or if it was just a queer-in-the-headlights thing last night."

Sonny snorted, shaking his head. "And?"

"Oh, I'm definitely a queer caught in the headlights."

Sonny blushed, the color creeping along the sides of his neck and up into his cheeks and ears. Abe wanted to feel the obvious heat there, against his face, his lips.

"Is that a new joke, or one of your greatest hits?"

"I don't know. Is that the blush of a guy who's uncomfortable, or charmed?"

Sonny's smile touched his eyes as he averted them. "Just been a while."

"Would you like to go on a date with me, Sonny?"

Sonny met his eyes. "Really?"

Abe searched his face playfully. "Is that a sarcastic really or a sincere really?"

"Sincere," Sonny said. "I don't do sarcastic well."

Abe found himself looking at Sonny's lips, then back up at his eyes. "So, would you?"

"When?"

"Is that a depends-when when, or an absolutely when?"

"Do you always ask so many questions?"

Abe put his hands up. "What can I say? I'm a cop."

"All right, Officer. For the record, it's an absolutely when. Now, when?"

"Tomorrow night? I can pick you up."

Sonny finished off his water. "Sounds like a date. See you then."

Abe watched him go, not caring who saw him do it.

* * *

Sonny smiled the whole way home. At first, he was convinced Abe was trying to somehow figure out if Sonny was to blame for the vandalism. He didn't understand how he could be responsible for it, but that was all he could think. Yet when he'd confronted the notion head on, Abe had softened. And the flirting, that was real.

He felt the heat in his cheeks, felt the way his body reacted. He wouldn't say that Abe was exactly his type, but Abe was likely everyone's type in some way. The longish blond hair he wore loose, some falling over his brow, complementing his blue eyes perfectly. His infectious smile, not only making whoever it was aimed at smile back, but flush under the warmth of it.

He shifted in his seat, chuckling at himself.

Sonny had the following day off from the bar. Trying not to focus too much on the time, or how nervous he was, he was relieved when Leigh called.

"What happened to calling every day?" she teased, but he could imagine she was genuinely let down by the lack of communication on his part.

"I'm sorry. It's been a little much here, getting settled in and everything." He hadn't told his family about the vandalism and hoped he wouldn't have to.

"Yeah, sure. Met any cute guys?"

"Why, have you?"

"Answering a question with a question." She tutted. "Classic deflection."

"Very funny. How're Mom and Maddy?"

"Maddy's fine. Mom's been bugging the shit out of me. 'Have you heard from your brother? How is he?'" she mimicked their mother's voice playfully.

"And?"

"And until now, I've had to tell her no."

"I'm fine." His eyes fell on the can of leftover paint next to the door leading from the kitchen to the garage.

"Really?"

"Really." He sighed. "I have a date tonight."

"Shut up, no you don't!"

He couldn't help but smile. It was nice to have people excited for him instead of worrying about him. "I do, actually."

"Well, I won't ask about him until you've had a few dates, but start taking notes. I want a full report if it becomes a thing."

"Yes, ma'am."

"Hey, Sonny?"

He heard the shift in her voice to serious, and leaned against the kitchen counter. "Yeah, Leigh?"

"Just, take care of yourself. Okay?"

It broke his heart that Leigh had to say that, that his little sister had to worry about him. "I promise. You too."

"With Maddy right here and Mom breathing down my neck? I don't have much of a choice," she joked.

"Love you."

"Love you too. Have fun on your *date*!" She drew out the last word like any good little sister would before hanging up.

* * *

Abe pulled up beside Sonny's truck in the driveway and parked. He studied the garage door and couldn't even make out a shadow where the damage had been. He wished he could get away with walking right up to it and inspecting it, but he thought Sonny might not appreciate that. Especially since he'd already caught Abe red-handed in wondering if Sonny could've done it himself. Which meant he either did do it himself, or he was incredibly perceptive. Abe couldn't dismiss either option until he knew Sonny better.

He got out of his car and walked up to the front door. He knocked, feeling the slow creep of his nerves.

After a moment, Sonny opened the door.

"Shucks," Abe said, leaning against the doorframe.

"And here I was beginning to think you were gonna make me use my cop knock."

Sonny smiled and, as it had the night before, it lit up his entire face. "You know, I have noticed that when you're not asking a bunch of questions, you throw out these ridiculously flirty jokes."

Abe smirked. "Well, they work, don't they?" He moved so Sonny could shut the door and lock it behind him.

"The questions or the jokes?" Sonny asked, seemingly serious, but the smile and the color in his cheeks gave him away.

"Do you try to be that cute?"

"Not as hard as you do."

Abe whistled, walking him to his car.

"I, uh, I kinda thought I'd drive."

Abe shrugged. "Suit yourself."

They climbed into Sonny's truck, and he started it. Suddenly, the cab was filled with classic rock. Specifically, the band Queen, revving up one of their hits.

Abe eyed Sonny as he buckled himself in.

"What?"

"Aren't you a little young for Queen?"

Sonny chuckled, backing out of his driveway and onto the road. "They're my favorite."

"You're kidding."

"Nope. Pretty sure Freddie was my first love."

Abe laughed, not at him, but at the idea of an even younger Sonny idolizing the deceased rocker. "You know, maybe I can imagine that."

"Who was yours?"

Abe frowned playfully. "Mine?"

"Yeah. Or, wait, are you one of those jerks who 'isn't

into music'?"

Abe smiled. "Jon Bon Jovi." Sonny beamed at that, and Abe was sure he was going to tease him for it.

"You know, that's interesting because you favor him a bit."

"Shut up," Abe said, looking out the window as he felt himself blush.

They went to a small bar/restaurant combo in Corpus Christi, in the younger, recently gentrified part of town. While Abe knew that, he also knew that in this part of the city, they were less likely to be harassed. It was coming along, but there were still awful things happening in the South, as evidenced by Sonny's recent experience.

They sat across from each other at a bar table. Abe had ordered a light beer and Sonny a seltzer water.

"One beer wouldn't kill ya," Abe ribbed him.

"I'm out with a cop," he tossed back.

Abe fanned his hands out. "Fair enough. So, what brought you to Sweetshade?"

"Just needed a change of scenery. I'm from Maryland. Lived there my whole life." *Except for...*

"I've lived here my whole life, if that isn't completely obvious," Abe said.

"You don't twang, but you do draw a bit at times," Sonny remarked.

"Thank'ye," Abe said with a wink.

Sonny shook his head. "I was in the military. The army, actually. One tour in Afghanistan. But it wasn't really for me, I guess."

Abe saw his face fall, saw the sadness pass through his eyes that made him look closer to his twenty-six years than he normally did. "Sometimes it's not. But you're young. You've got plenty of time to figure out where you're going in life."

"Yeah," Sonny said.

Their drinks came, and they ordered their meals. Steak and baked potato for Abe, garden salad dressed in oil and vinegar for Sonny.

"You could have more than salad," Abe said.

"I, uh, actually can't here."

Abe frowned.

"I'm vegan," Sonny explained.

"So, wait, let me get this straight. You're a military man. You go to church. You don't eat meat, and you rarely drink. And you look like this too?"

Sonny smiled, though he was clearly embarrassed.

Abe leaned back in his seat. "Do you save kittens from trees as well?"

"Ha-ha."

"If I see you help an old lady across the street, I'm gonna have to call bullshit."

* * *

Sonny could still feel Abe sizing him up, could feel the dissatisfaction when he didn't go any deeper into his past.

"Can I ask a direct question?"

Abe chewed a piece of steak, not looking up at him. "Sure."

"You and Nate, Officer Landis, you guys think I did it, don't you?"

Abe stopped. He put his knife and fork down and wiped his mouth. He then met Sonny's eyes. "We've considered it."

Sonny sighed, sitting back from the table, hands in

his lap. "That's why you asked me out, isn't it?" When Abe didn't immediately answer, Sonny felt desperate. "It wasn't me. I swear it. Come on, you're gay. Do you really think I'd do that? To myself?"

Abe leaned forward. "For the record, I don't."

Sonny narrowed his eyes.

"Okay, maybe I did a little last night when I came in again. But" — he shook his head — "it just doesn't fit."

"Am I stupid for thinking you liked me?"

Abe seemed to hear the disappointment in Sonny's voice, and suddenly he was reaching across the table for Sonny's hand. "No, you're not."

Sonny peered up at him cautiously, not pulling away.

Abe smiled. "Come on, you have to know you're handsome. And sweet. And funny. Plus, you're the only other gay guy in town that I know of. We have to go on at least one date. It's the law."

Sonny snickered. "Really?" he asked incredulously, arching an eyebrow.

"Look, I don't make the laws. But as one of Sweetshade's finest, it is my job to enforce them." Abe squeezed his hand once before releasing it.

"Well, heaven knows I don't want to go breaking any laws," he said as Abe sat back again, the tension easing between them.

"You? Never," Abe said, then took another drink of his beer.

* * *

The drive back to Sonny's house was quieter, one of the rock radio stations playing low as they rode along. Abe

70

sensed the lingering tension between them, though most of it had dissipated after they'd spoken candidly.

He walked Sonny to his door.

"Thanks for dinner," Sonny said. "And the laughs."

"You have a great laugh," Abe remarked.

"But your jokes? Meh," he said, his hand wavering in the air.

Abe nudged him in the ribs. "Without mine, where would you get setups for yours?"

Sonny looked down at him. "True."

Abe felt it then, watched as Sonny looked him in the eyes, then down at his lips briefly. "Are you waiting for me to set you up now?"

"Abe," Sonny said.

"Because if you need me to—"

"Abel." His full name on Sonny's lips stopped him in his tracks, made him sense what Sonny was about to do just before he did it.

"S-Sonny," he said, just as Sonny closed the space between them, touching his lips to Abe's. Sonny kissed him once, twice. "I don't even know what Sonny is short for," he murmured between Sonny's kisses, almost forgetting it was a lie.

"Harrison," Sonny whispered, lips brushing the corner of Abe's mouth.

How many lies are you going to tell him? he chastised himself, but as goose bumps rose along his arms and sides, his attraction outweighed his guilt. "Harrison," Abe said, smiling.

"Mm-hm," Sonny hummed, nuzzling back into another kiss.

Abe let him, resting his hands on Sonny's waist. Sonny wasn't a small man. He was a head taller than Abe and fit; there was certainly more of him than there was of Abe. *A substantial man with a substantial, sexy name.* He felt himself melt a little. He rubbed his thumbs against Sonny's sides, felt the quiver beneath the fabric as he did. *Sweet Sonny.*

Sonny broke the kiss, pulling back slightly.

"No, come back," Abe said softly.

Sonny cupped his face, peering down into his eyes. "As much as I'm enjoying making out with you on my front porch, I kinda feel like I'm taunting whoever did that to my garage."

"Piss on them," Abe said.

"Easy for you to say," Sonny replied, his hands dropping to Abe's shoulders. "Officer Ellis."

"Do you at least believe me now?"

Sonny frowned, confused.

"That I like you and I wasn't just being a shithead cop, asking you on a date with ulterior motives?"

"Aw, no ulterior motives? None? And here I thought you said I was cute."

"Well, I mean, I usually don't even kiss on the first date, so…" He trailed off. *What is it about this kid?* He then remembered the haunted look that'd passed over his otherwise handsome, youthful features when he'd spoken of his service. *Man,* he corrected himself.

"Me neither, to be honest," Sonny admitted.

"Well, I'll get going like the gentleman I am, then."

Sonny held him for a moment, lifting a hand to brush Abe's hair from his eyes.

"Nate says I should cut it."

"Don't you dare," Sonny said.

Abe felt his cheeks heat.

"This isn't the last time, right? We'll do this again?"

Sonny asked the question with such hope in his eyes that Abe melted a bit more.

"Hell yes," Abe said. "Like I said, it's the law."

Sonny chuckled as they released each other. "Fair enough. I'll text you later."

"All right. Thanks, Sonny."

* * *

Sonny unlocked his door as Abe descended the porch steps, heading for his car.

"Have a good night!" Sonny called over his shoulder. He let himself into the house, riding the afterglow of their date and parting kisses, turning to lean his back against the closed door...and was promptly sobered by the chaos before him.

Broken glass littered the floor, the side kitchen door standing ajar. Though his house didn't appear to be completely ransacked, it was clear someone had broken in and went through it. The hair stood up on the back of his neck and arms as he wondered if someone was still in the house.

He opened the front door and stepped outside, hoping Abe would still be there.

* * *

Abe was just about to reverse out of the driveway and head home when he saw Sonny come out of the house, white as a ghost.

"Shit," he swore, throwing his car into park. He reached into his glove box and retrieved his revolver before getting out of his car. "Sonny!"

"I-I think someone broke in."

Abe came around the car and jogged up the steps. "Stay out here and call nine-one-one," he said before proceeding into Sonny's house, gun drawn.

* * *

For a jumpy ex-military man, Harrison Lakes seemed awfully naive to him. No motion sensors, no security alarm, not even proper locks on his doors. All he'd had to do was break the glass to the side door and let himself in.

He'd looked around the house, somewhat taken aback by how normal it was, almost dull in its plainness. Nothing interesting in the kitchen or living room, other than the fact that Lakes seemed to prefer music to television. Vinyl records far outnumbered the available TV stations he had. What few books he found were mostly nonfiction, mixed with a little Stephen King. That was when he spotted a well-worn copy of the Bible, with dog-eared pages and sticky notes marking specific passages. He sneered at that, hate boiling inside him. Only, it wasn't hatred. It was something far fouler and more potent than hate. He was just about to take it – maybe as a trophy *– when he heard them return.*

Them.

Lakes and that queer cop, Ellis.

And then Ellis was escorting Lakes to his door. Like the perfect gentleman fag. He'd been ready to split, when the men stopped on the front porch, murmuring to each other. He couldn't hear them, but he could tell by the smiles and flushed cheeks that they were flirting with each other. Kissing followed, and he felt his skin crawl. Lakes seemed to be the only one with any sense then, pulling away when clearly it was the last thing either wanted.

He'd seen enough. He quietly left through the same door he'd used to break into the house, sneaking away into the night before Lakes ever let himself into his house.

Seven

Abe checked the house thoroughly, level by level, basement, ground floor, and upstairs. Rooms, closets, even behind things, and found no one. Someone had definitely been there, no question. It almost looked like they'd been looking for something. He'd seen robberies and how ransacked a place could look. The lack of that was almost chilling in and of itself.

When he came back out, Nate had shown up and was speaking with Sonny, who looked upset.

"I told you, I don't know who might've done this," Sonny said, exasperated.

The tension between them eased slightly when Abe approached.

"No one inside. I checked everywhere," Abe said, tucking his gun into the back of his jeans.

"And you're sure you locked up when you left?"

"Yes," Sonny snapped.

"Nate, I watched him do it."

"All doors?"

"Well, no, but I was with him the whole time."

"He thinks I did it before we left," Sonny said.

Nate threw his hands up. "I didn't say that."

"You don't have to. You asked me what happened, and I told you how it looked. You asked me who I thought did it, and I told you — for the second time — that I don't know. I barely know anyone around here." Sonny ran a hand through his hair. "I'm not doing it, and I'm not making it up."

"Calm down, Sonny," Abe said.

"I came here to start over. To have a life and—" He stopped, shaking his head.

"Start over from what? You said things back home were fine, that you were just looking for a change."

Abe shot Nate a look.

"What? It's a valid question, Officer Ellis."

"He was white as a sheet when he came back out. I saw it—"

"No, you saw a pair of pretty blue eyes and lost your perspective."

"Excuse me?"

Nate huffed, turning his attention back to Sonny. "Look, I don't know what's going on here, but when it involves my best friend, I fucking care." Abe watched Sonny and Nate lock eyes, watched Sonny for any change in his face. There was nothing, save for the increasing despair etched into the set of his jaw and mouth.

"I understand that. But it's not me. I don't know what else I have to do or say to prove it."

"Come on, Nate, leave him alone."

Nate looked back and forth between them, clearly unsatisfied. "I'm watching you, Sonny."

"F-fine," Sonny said before retreating into his house.

* * *

Sonny was sweeping up the glass in the kitchen when he heard a knock at the front door.

"It's just me," Abe called.

"Door's open," Sonny called back. He continued

cleaning up the broken shards, even when he saw Abe appear in the doorway in his peripheral vision.

"Want some help?"

"No."

Apparently, Abe didn't take that to heart because, instead, he knelt and placed a hand on Sonny's shoulder. "Let me help you."

Sonny jerked away from his touch. "No. I'm dangerous, remember? Unstable. Doing it for attention or whatever he thinks." He could feel Abe's eyes on him, just like he'd been able to feel his mother's. And sisters'. And Dr. Ford's. And everyone else's since he'd come home.

"You know I don't think that," Abe said gently.

There's that tone. It crawled over his skin like a too-gentle touch, irritating him instead of soothing.

"I don't know what you think."

"Sonny…"

"What?" he snapped. He could see how uncomfortable Abe was. *Yeah, because you're acting like an ass right now.*

But instead of throwing his hands up in surrender and leaving, Abe held Sonny's eyes. "I don't think you did this, and I don't think you spray-painted your garage. I don't know what you've been through or what you're still going through, but I want to be your friend if nothing else. I want to help you, but you have to let me."

He'd heard the speech a thousand times, a thousand different ways, but when Abe said it, he could almost believe it.

He wants to help. He likes you. Those kisses were real. And when you were scared, he came running. He barely knows you, and he came running, literally guns blazing.

Yeah, because I've never clocked him in the face for

startling me awake. What happens when he sees the real me?

"I don't need your help," Sonny said, turning back to the task of cleaning up glass. He focused hard, even when Abe stood up and left. He listened for his car to start, listened as he pulled away from Sonny's house and drove off.

* * *

Abe had meant to drive straight home, but in his frustration, he turned for the police station. He parked and slammed the car door behind him. He charged through the back door and found Nate at his desk.

"Great. Here we go." Nate closed the file he'd been looking at, then sat back in his chair.

"Yeah, here we go," Abe said. "What the hell was that?"

"What do you mean, what was that?"

"I was with him all evening. I watched him lock the door behind him, and we had a nice dinner. He wasn't upset or stressed at all. I don't know why you've got a bug up your ass about him, but—"

"You watched him lock the *front* door. The damage was done to the side door, Abe."

Abe shrugged. "So? Like I said, he wasn't stressed or anxious."

"He wouldn't be if he's the one who set it up."

Abe scrubbed a hand over his face. "Look, he's got an interesting past. I get that. But he genuinely seems like a good guy." Nate looked away, shaking his head. "Come on, don't my instincts count for anything?"

"You know he's got a history of violence, right?"

"What do you mean?"

Nate motioned him over. "The Maryland Police says he was admitted to a psychiatric ward not only due to his suicide attempt, but also—look at this." He handed a file to Abe, pointing to a particular section they hadn't read through the first time they looked at the report.

Abe frowned. "I don't understand."

"He hit his mother in the face, it says here. She 'startled' him."

Abe read the report, a pit growing in his stomach. He didn't want to believe it, even as he compared the information to the way Sonny had snapped at him.

"One incident doesn't make a history of violence, Nate. Plus, he's a veteran. Maybe he's just jumpy," Abe reasoned.

"Maybe. And maybe he's got a short fuse, Abe. I'm just trying to see it from all angles."

Abe slumped in his desk chair, running both hands through his hair.

"Look, I don't give a shit who you date. But I don't want you to get tangled up with someone who's unstable to the point of being violent."

"Noted," Abe said. "But I'm a big boy. I can look out for myself, and something's telling me it isn't him, that report notwithstanding."

* * *

Sonny tossed and turned most of the night, despite staying up to thoroughly clean the downstairs and temporarily repairing the damage to the side door until he could call someone about it.

He'd lain in bed, angry and dejected, fighting with himself. The date with Abe had gone so well, and it'd felt so good—so normal—to go out with someone. And the glow he'd gotten from kissing him had been thrilling and grounding in equal measures. He'd spent so long and so much energy trying to get his head on straight, he'd nearly forgotten about the part of him that longed for affection and companionship. Those needs had seemed secondary when he'd been so focused on building some semblance of normalcy in this new place. He'd had just a taste, and it'd been yanked away from him.

It's not fair.

When did fair *ever apply to you, Sonny boy?*

He pushed himself upright and turned on the bedside lamp, shoving the depressing truth from his mind. Tired and cranky, he looked around his room.

Did they even take anything, or just went through my shit and made a mess while they were at it? Nothing seemed to be missing. He kept everything of value locked in a safe, which hadn't been touched during the break-in. He'd checked his books and albums, not that anyone would want his worn paperbacks or ratty old records.

So, what did they want?

He rubbed his hands over his arms, feeling violated, even though it appeared nothing had been taken from him.

The following day, at his wits' end, Sonny reached out to Daniel, who agreed to meet with him. Sonny sat at the same table at the Sweet Bean, waiting for him.

He came alone this time, and Sonny was grateful. He was under enough stress without having to deal with self-righteous teenage angst.

Daniel ordered his drink, then joined Sonny at his table. "Sonny," he said, shaking his hand.

"Thanks for meeting with me again," he said, and Daniel must've sensed something amiss.

"Of course. You seem a little down. What's the matter?"

"I, uh, I seem to have an issue with harassment. Someone keeps doing things to my house."

Daniel took the lid off his coffee and stirred it. "I've heard."

Sonny looked up at him, alarmed.

"Small town," he said.

Sonny averted his gaze, feeling frustrated and embarrassed. "I guess you know about the spray-painting, then."

Daniel nodded. "I'm so sorry."

"You said you thought Sweetshade was fairly accepting."

"It is, at least from what I gather. Officer Ellis and his brother, Richard, never seemed to have an issue."

Sonny felt mildly taken aback, although he knew it made sense for Abe's orientation to be known. He'd lived here his whole life, he'd said.

"Have you met Abe?"

"I have."

"He's been good to this town, for this town. I think everyone was kind of surprised when he stuck around, after what happened with his brother."

"What happened?"

"Richard was a little rougher around the edges. Committed some armed robberies a while back. He's been in Huntsville for the past, gosh, six years? Eight? I can't remember."

"I just don't understand who's doing this. I don't know anyone. I haven't told anyone except for a couple of people."

"Sonny, it's a small town. It's a nice small town, but it's still a small town."

Sonny sighed.

Daniel looked concerned. "I don't either, to be honest. We've never really had anything like this, aside from Rich's robberies. And those weren't targeting anyone in particular. Things stay pretty quiet here."

"Should I stop coming to your church? I don't want to cause any trouble," he said, his tone heavy with regret.

Daniel shook his head. "Absolutely not."

"I don't want to make anyone uncomfortable, and I can't help but think I have," he admitted.

"You don't come to church for other people, son," Daniel said firmly. "You come for God and yourself. That's it."

Oh yeah? And where exactly has God been these past few years? he thought bitterly.

"I know it's difficult right now, but this is when it counts."

"I guess so. I just feel lost."

Daniel reached across the table and touched Sonny's arm. Not in an overbearing way, but in the way his own father had so many times when Sonny struggled. When he'd come out, when he'd decided he wanted to join the army, when his father had shown the first signs of heart disease. Each time, his father had reached out—whether to wrap an arm around his shoulders or pull him into a hug—to reassure his only son that he was more than capable of defeating whatever battle he happened to be fighting. He hadn't realized how much he missed it until right then.

"That's when your faith counts. Don't be afraid to

lean into it."

"I feel like he's not hearing me," Sonny said.

"Sometimes faith can be blind. Sometimes it has to be. But he's still there, Sonny. He's always there."

Sonny nodded, feeling himself getting choked up. "You're right. I'm sorry, you're absolutely right."

"It's okay to be unsure," Daniel said. "God understands that much more than people think. He's asking you to trust and believe, not demanding it."

"Thank you," he said.

Daniel withdrew his hand and took a drink of his coffee. Sonny followed suit, managing to stifle the lingering tears that had threatened only moments ago.

"Of course. I'm glad you reached out to me."

Sonny sat back in his chair, taking another drink of his black coffee. "Like I said, I don't know too many people around here. I just wanted to know what you thought."

"I don't know what to think of what's been happening to you. But I'm sorry for it. I'd expected better from Sweetshade."

Sonny shrugged. "Maybe it's just because I'm new. Maybe they're done now."

Daniel nodded. "I hope so."

Once home, Sonny called a window repair company. He was in the process of installing deadbolts on the exterior doors when his smartphone pinged in his back pocket. He stopped and checked it.

I thought you'd text me later, Abe had sent.

Sonny felt his adrenaline spike, not having expected that Abe would want to speak to him after the way he'd behaved the night before.

I'm sorry.

It was all he could think to write.

Do you want me to buzz off?

Sonny knew he should tell him yes. He knew nothing good could come of continuing to pursue a relationship. He also knew how juvenile it would be to tell Abe through a text message.

Let's talk. Maybe one of our places, unless that's too uncomfortable?

Sonny fully expected to be shot down, or at least told he'd rather meet in a public place. But he didn't.

Yours. I'd like to help you look into some better security measures after we talk.

Sonny was browsing the Internet for home security systems when Abe showed up, knocking on the front screen door. Sonny came to the door, unlatched it, and let him in.

"Hey," Abe said. "I'm glad you didn't just yell 'door's open' again." It was an attempt at teasing that fell miserably flat. "Sorry."

"It's fine," Sonny said. He sat on the arm of his couch, while Abe stood awkwardly in the foyer area.

Abe scratched the back of his neck. "You wanted to talk?"

Sonny swallowed thickly. "I don't think we should be doing this."

"Doing what?"

"This. Us. I'm not really in a good place right now," Sonny explained, trying not to cringe from embarrassment. *It's not you, it's me.*

"Look at me," Abe said.

Sonny made himself meet Abe's eyes.

"If that's what you want, then that's okay. We don't have to continue seeing each other. But if you think you don't deserve to date someone because of what's happening to you or what you're going through, I'm going to have to call bullshit."

"What if Nate's right?"

"About what?"

"What if I'm putting you in danger? I mean, I know he thinks I'm the one doing this. I'm not. But all the same, someone broke into my house last night. I don't know who or why." He faltered, looking down at his hands, which he'd begun to wring nervously. "I don't want anyone to get hurt because of me." *There's been enough of that,* he thought, and it tore at him.

"Sonny," Abe said, coming closer. "You're not a curse."

Sonny clenched his jaw, grinding his teeth against the emotion triggered by those words. He shook his head. "You barely know me."

"Like I said, I'm not going to push or pressure you. If you want me to leave you alone, I will. But I'm not going to do it because you think it's what you deserve."

Sonny nodded, relieved. "I swear, this isn't me."

"I know it's not." Abe cupped his face in his hands, and Sonny peered up at him.

"How?"

"I just do. I've been a cop long enough. And..." He seemed to think back on something. A painful memory perhaps. "I just know when someone's lying or slipping, even if we're close. And you're not."

Sonny raised his hands and pressed them over Abe's, turning to kiss the edge of one palm. "Thank you."

Abe leaned in and pressed a kiss to the top of Sonny's

head. "All right. Now show me what you've done to secure the place."

Sonny popped up and walked Abe to each exterior door, showing him the new deadbolts. Abe approved, stopping to inspect the breached door more carefully than the others.

"There was glass all over your kitchen floor?"

Sonny nodded. "The doorframe and door were fine for the most part. I think they just broke the window and reached inside. N-not that I'd know. I'm just guessing. Because of the glass."

Abe smirked. "I know, Sonny. I know you didn't do it."

Sonny sighed heavily. "Nate would've hung me for that for sure."

"Probably," Abe said. "It's good you got the keyed lock on both sides for all doors. It wouldn't stop them from breaking a window and climbing in, but it would slow them down if they tried their original method again."

"That's what I read."

"Very good. Have you thought about a security system?"

"I was actually reading online about them when you came. Just narrowing down based on reviews."

"I'd recommend an alarm, possibly motion sensors. I'd say cameras too, but I don't know what kind of budget you're working with. And one more thing." He picked up the small black case he'd placed on the table next to the door when he'd come in. "I want you to have this."

"A gun?"

Abe nodded.

"No. No, I don't want a gun."

Abe stopped, confused. "You're a military man; you know how they work."

"You're right, I do. I don't want one in my house."

His eyes fixed on the case. He knew it was probably just a small, basic handgun, but he still couldn't bear it. Not with his mental health in the state it was in.

"Hey." Abe reached out and touched his shoulder. He seemed to feel the flinch Sonny barely managed to stifle, his hand dropping away at once. "It's okay. It was just a thought."

"I'm not, like, anti-gun. I just..."

"You don't have to explain." Abe placed it back on the table next to the door. "Not unless you want to. And besides, I saw the set of knives in your kitchen. You should be okay." Sonny relaxed a little.

Abe came to him and wrapped his arms loosely around Sonny's waist.

"I'm sorry," Sonny said, laying his arms over Abe's, his hands against Abe's back.

"Don't be."

"No, I am. I-I'm still dealing with some stuff. But that's not an excuse to snap at you like I did last night."

"Sonny..."

"I'm working on it, though. That's why I moved here. I wanted to start over, you know?"

Abe nodded. "It was just a bump. A forgivable bump."

Eight

To Sonny's surprise, no one seemed to agree with Nate about his questionable innocence. He and Abe made plans for dinner at Sonny's house Sunday evening. Daniel had reassured him, and even restored his faith a little. He hadn't been to therapy in a couple of weeks, but all things considered, he felt he was doing fairly well. Even Jean was still friendly toward him at work.

"I was sorry to hear what happened," she said as he wiped down the bar. "And sorry for how Nate acted."

Sonny shot her a look. "What? You don't think I did it to myself?" He asked it with a wink, but she remained serious.

"No, I don't," she said firmly. "I think you've gotten close to his best friend, and he doesn't know you, so he's skeptical."

"Skeptical would be asking a few questions about me, not all out accusing me of lying," Sonny said. He hadn't meant to be argumentative, but it slipped out. "I'm sorry. It's just…" He shook his head. "I wouldn't do that. If I'd wanted someone to breathe down my neck and watch my every move, I'd have stayed in Maryland with my family."

She snickered. "That bad?"

"My father passed away a while back. But my mom and sisters more than make up for it, believe me."

"No brothers?"

"Nope."

"Poor thing." She nudged his shoulder. "I know I'm sleeping with the enemy, as they say, but I'm still your friend if you ever need to talk."

He nodded. "I know. And he's not the enemy. I get it. New guy comes to town and starts dating your best friend while all this weird stuff starts happening. I guess I'd be suspicious too."

"But Abe's a big boy. He can take care of himself, and he will, believe me."

Sonny chuckled. "I have no doubt."

"Whole lot of punch packed into that little guy, huh?"

"He's not exactly little," he said.

"I don't need, nor do I want to know," she said, putting her hands up in playful refusal.

"Not what I meant," he said, blushing, even as he took the joke in stride. "Jean, has this kind of thing ever happened here before? In Sweetshade?"

"Not that I know of, not openly. Some kids are shitheads to each other, but I've not seen this kind of thing here before."

Sonny chewed his lip. "I just don't get it. I haven't been here long enough to piss someone off. And even if I had, I'm the most boring person I know. I work here, I go to church, I go home. The one date Abe and I ever went on was out of town, and the harassment started before that anyhow."

Jean seemed to think it over, coming up empty. "And you're not loud. I mean, no shame if you wanted to be, but I guess I could see some folks around here being put off if you were. But you're not, about anything."

Sonny sighed. "I just wish I understood."

"I wish it'd stop."

"That too. But man, if I could at least know why or what I was doing. This kind of thing didn't happen to me back home either, or I'd think I'd brought it with me."

"It really makes no sense because everyone knows about Abe, and he's way more outspoken about it. And his brother, Rich, was openly bi. No one ever really gave him shit about it either."

Sonny looked over at her. "What happened with his brother?"

She arched an eyebrow. "I'd rather let Abe tell that tale."

He held up his hands in mock-surrender. "Fair enough. He's just come up a few times, and everyone gets that look on their face."

"Yeah..." She trailed off, clearly unwilling to divulge any further information. "But listen, I've got your back. Personally, I think Nate's wrong. I think Abe's instincts are good enough that if he thought you were doing this, he'd find out how and why and bring you in himself. If he trusts you, then I trust that. Because, darlin', you're cute, but you're not that cute."

Sonny laughed. "Got it."

* * *

Sunday evening came, and Abe was excited and eager to see Sonny again now that they'd cleared the air. He approached Sonny's door, glad to see the motion sensor light at the top right-hand corner of the porch awning. *Good boy.*

He knocked, and Sonny came to the door and let him in.

"Hey," Sonny said, smiling, the clouds in his eyes from their previous evening together completely dissolved.

Abe stepped inside, face heating when Sonny leaned in to kiss his cheek.

"Hey!" he said, grabbing his arm gently. "I haven't seen you in days. I think a proper kiss is in order."

Sonny beamed, leaning in to kiss him, and Abe kissed back, pressing against lips a bit fuller and softer than his own. *You're already a goner if you're internal-monologuing about his lips there, Abe.*

"Better?" Sonny whispered.

"For now." He cleared his throat. "So what's for dinner?"

"For you, steak."

Abe gaped at him. "Isn't that, like, against the rules?"

Sonny led the way into the kitchen, and Abe followed, then leaned against the doorframe.

"Yeah, but I wasn't sure about your stance on tofu or mock-meats in general."

"Mock-meats? What the fuck is a mock-meat?"

Sonny chuckled, tending to the separate pans, one containing Abe's steak, the other containing chopped and somehow doctored tofu. "You know, veggie burgers, fake chicken tenders."

"I mean, I'll try anything once. But I've never had stuff like that."

"Are you allergic to soy?"

"Not that I know of."

Sonny smiled. "Maybe next time, then."

Abe warmed at the idea of a next time. And maybe more next times after that. "You still know how to cook a steak, though?"

Sonny gave him a look that Abe found both humorous and incredibly charming. "I wasn't born vegan."

"Well, I don't know how they do it in Maryland."

"I listened to how you ordered the other night. And saw you were mildly annoyed when your steak came out a little too done."

Abe had to stop himself from biting his lip. "It was a little done. Still fine, but…"

"But you'd like it to bleed just a little more than that."

"So, you're not a regular vegan. You're a cool vegan."

"I respect your decision to eat the way you do. All I ask is for the same respect in return."

Abe smiled at that. "Gee, Sonny, are you saving yourself for marriage too?"

"No. I'm not." He looked over at Abe with playful heat in his eyes.

Abe felt warmth creep into his cheeks, expanding toward his throat and chest. "Just when I think you're this Goody Two-shoes…" He trailed off, shaking his head.

Just a few minutes later, they sat down together at Sonny's dining-room table.

"Medium-cooked steak, mushrooms and onions, and sautéed mixed greens," Sonny said, setting their plates down.

"What's yours?"

"The same, except I'm having sautéed tofu."

"Looks perfect."

They ate for several moments in silence.

"Good?"

Abe nodded. "Perfect. Way better than that place. Which we won't be going back to. I felt awful when you only had salad."

"Don't. When in doubt, there's always french fries and salad."

"So, these veggies, they're vegan?"

"Uh, yeah."

Abe rolled his eyes. "No, I mean, how you cooked them, smart-ass."

Sonny took a drink of his beer. "Yep. Olive oil, salt, and pepper. Nothing too crazy."

Abe narrowed his eyes playfully. "Is this how you vegans get us? By lulling us into a false sense of security?"

Sonny snapped his fingers. "Damn. You caught me."

Abe laughed. This was when he was sure Sonny would make a good partner—when he was relaxed and bantering right along with him. He took a long pull of his beer. "How's yours?"

"Why? Want to try it?"

"Sure."

Sonny speared a piece of tofu, gathering a few veggies to give it the full effect, and held it out for Abe.

Abe leaned forward and took the bite directly from Sonny's fork. He could feel Sonny watching him and realized how suggestive what he was doing was. He'd meant to flirt, but suddenly felt like he'd crossed a weird line. He sat back, chewing the bite and trying not to blush again. "Okay, a little weird, but not bad. Not meat, but— wait, is tofu a mock-meat?"

"No. It's a protein source in its own right, made from soy."

"Hmm," Abe murmured as he chewed and swallowed. "Really not bad. I always thought of tofu as those squishy blocks in the produce section that, I'm sorry, creep me out."

"Well, you have to prepare it. You wouldn't just take

a raw piece of meat and eat it."

Abe chuckled. "True."

After dinner, they sat on Sonny's couch, each enjoying a second beer and some music. Sonny had a TV, but he didn't have cable, and frankly, Abe didn't want to watch TV anyway. He could do that at home.

"You're a hell of a cook," Abe said, turning to face Sonny.

"I was hoping so. After everything last time, I just wanted us to be able to relax."

Abe felt himself wanting to touch him, to soothe away the leftover anxiety he could hear in his voice. "I know. But you're safe. We're safe. You've updated your security, and you're with a cop."

Sonny turned to him then, a smile tugging at the corners of his lips. "That's true."

Abe lifted a hand, gently touching Sonny's face with the backs of two fingers, tracing his cheekbone.

Sonny let out a breath, thick black lashes fluttering.

"You're safe with me."

"I want you to be safe with me," Sonny said, his brow furrowing.

"Ah-ah, hey, relax," Abe said, scooting closer. Sonny opened his eyes. "Just because you're bigger and probably stronger doesn't mean you have to be the one to bear all the burden."

Sonny bit his bottom lip, seeming to take that to heart. He leaned in and pressed his lips to Abe's.

Abe basked in the warm glow of Sonny's hard-won trust. *Okay, maybe not complete trust, maybe not yet. But we're headed in the right direction –*

His thoughts were cut off when Sonny reached over and pulled him into his lap. Abe straddled his thighs, wrapping his arms loosely around Sonny's neck and shoulders. He took in the sight of Sonny's flushed cheeks and full lips, made even fuller from kissing. "You enjoy that, don't you?"

"What?" Sonny asked.

"Being able to pick me up and move me at will," Abe said.

Sonny nuzzled against Abe's jaw, pressing kisses there. "Maybe I do. And I think you enjoy it too."

Abe leaned into his kisses, feeling the goose bumps they induced. "You're right."

Sonny snorted, and Abe felt his breath against his throat, warm and laced with laughter. His hands slid down over Abe's bottom, squeezing him and pulling them flush together.

"S-Sonny," Abe breathed, rocking closer.

Sonny leaned back, looking up at him, leaving one arm wrapped around his back while the opposite hand reached up and brushed his hair back from his face.

"You know, you're a pretty guy, Abe," Sonny said, grazing his thumb back and forth against Abe's cheek.

Abe gripped Sonny's shoulders and playfully pinned him back. "Pretty, huh?"

"Mm-hm," Sonny hummed, seeming to know how it would razz Abe, and pushed his hips up against him. The movement made Abe moan before he could smother the noise. "You blush pretty. You make pretty noises."

"Very funny," Abe said, even as he felt his cheeks heating just as Sonny said.

Sonny smoothed his hands over Abe's back and bottom, almost petting him, and Abe couldn't take it any longer. He leaned back on his legs and began undoing Sonny's jeans. Sonny tensed for a second, seeming

95

uncertain.

"Let me?" Abe asked, waiting for permission.

After a beat, Sonny nodded, relaxing back against the couch.

Abe smiled, undoing Sonny's pants and reaching inside, freeing his erection. He held him, thick and hot and satisfyingly heavy in his hand. He stroked him once, watching Sonny relax the rest of the way. Abe stood, briefly taking in the sight, then knelt before him.

* * *

Sonny let himself be kissed, let Abe rub against him and touch him, returning the affections. But when Abe knelt in front of him, Sonny felt his body respond in a way it hadn't in a long time. Years, maybe. He wanted Abe, wanted what was coming, wanted even more.

Abe wrapped his hand around the base of Sonny's cock, leaned in, and rubbed his cheek against him, turning to drag his lips along the side.

"Abe," he breathed, feeling his soft lips and warm breath.

Abe sat back and took the tip into his mouth, sucking as he pulled back until it popped from between his lips. "Sweet Sonny," he murmured, tonguing the head.

Sonny ran his hands through Abe's blond hair, pushing the loose, messy strands back from his face, watching as he took him into his mouth again. But instead of pulling back, he pressed forward, taking as much of Sonny as he could. He worked at it, taking a little more each time until Sonny found himself completely embedded in Abe's mouth and throat.

"That feels s-so good," he hissed, blinded by

pleasure, his head falling back against the couch.

Abe continued to work at him, making the sexiest noises as he did. Sometimes they resembled moans, sometimes just wet sucking sounds. It didn't matter, because all of it sounded like sex, and Sonny hadn't realized just how much he'd been craving it. He leaned his cheek against his own shoulder, peering down at Abe through heavy eyes, watching him.

Abe must've sensed it because he looked up at him, stopping to tease at the head again with his tongue, winking as he did.

"You're trouble," Sonny said, although it came out more groan than anything.

"You bet, big guy." Abe winked, then returned to the task at hand. He turned his head, pressing wet, sucking kisses along the underside of Sonny's cock, making Sonny's thighs jump at the intense sensation, making him gasp. "I just adore you, you know that?"

Sonny threaded his fingers through Abe's hair. "I f-feel the same—*Oh!*" He cried out when Abe took him once more down his throat, nuzzling when he managed to get him fully seated, humming. "Oh Christ."

Abe began bobbing again, up and down in smooth, sustained motions, consuming Sonny over and over.

"Abe, I'm getting close," he panted, trying not to thrust.

Abe pulled off him, even though it was clear it was the last thing he wanted to do. "Go ahead, fuck," he murmured. "I can take it."

Sonny hesitated for a moment, but as Abe took him down his throat once again, he knew he was too far gone to object. His hips lifted, and Abe took it, opening his throat and letting Sonny have what his body had been fighting to restrain. He gripped Abe's hair and rocked, fucking his throat, taking his pleasure. Abe let him, holding on to his thighs, seeming to predict and account for his movements with angle and pressure.

"Oh f-fuck," Sonny swore as he came, pushing against the back of Abe's throat once, twice more before sagging back against the couch, sated, if slightly embarrassed.

Abe sat back on his heels, face flushed, hair tousled from Sonny's handling. But he smiled, eyes sparkling.

"You like that?" Sonny blurted out the question without thinking.

"You were so hot, fighting yourself. I couldn't resist," Abe said.

Sonny sat forward, reaching for him, pulling him into a kiss that tasted like sex and their mingled essence. And just when he was about to insist on reciprocity, his security alarm sounded with a deafening wail. "Ah!" Sonny cried, covering one ear.

"Shit," Abe swore, immediately sober and aware. "Stay in the house!" he shouted, coming to his feet.

"Where are you going?"

"To get my gun."

Sonny shoved himself back into his pants and did them up before silencing the alarm, all within the range of a minute. He peered out the open front door where Abe had gone, but only saw Abe coming back from his car.

"Stay inside, Sonny."

Sonny nodded as his smartphone began to ring, the security company calling him. He answered, giving them the verbal code before explaining the situation.

"N-no one broke in, but I think someone, or something, must've tripped one of the sensors," he explained.

"It looks like the sensor on the north side of the house was affected."

Sonny looked to the side window that faced the living room, the couch, and an eerie, sick feeling washed over him.

* * *

He'd been watching, all right. The sensor on the front porch made it too risky – he didn't want to be front and center on the porch if the alarm went off. He knew the second it did, that fag cop would come bounding out, eager to be the hero.

It'd come to his attention that Officer Ellis was eager in many ways, as he'd dropped to his knees in front of the newcomer, Lakes. It amazed him how brazen they'd been, going on their date, coming back and making out on the porch for all Sweetshade to see. And then, right there in the living room… He shuddered at what he'd seen them doing.

And to think he'd come to respect Ellis for how he'd kept his private life behind closed doors. Clearly, he'd been waiting to act on his vile urges until someone new came along.

He'd managed to get away just as the alarm began to sound, before the police arrived.

And why did you let it get that far?

Just standing in front of the window, perfectly still, hadn't been enough.

Because you leaned in when you saw that queer, Lakes, start bucking, and Ellis just taking it.

He cringed at his own curiosity, at his weakness.

Why? Do you really want to watch them fuck?

He hurried home, but not so quickly as to draw attention to himself.

Nine

Abe checked all around Sonny's house, but aside from confirming that it was indeed the north sensor that had been triggered, nothing looked disturbed. He found Sonny on the front porch, watching as Nate parked the police cruiser in front of the house.

Abe walked over and put his gun back in his car before coming to Sonny's side. "Just stay calm," he said under his breath. "You've got an airtight alibi this time." He noticed Sonny's hands holding on to the railing tight enough that his knuckles had gone white. Abe reached over and placed one hand over them.

Sonny looked over, and Abe saw the uneasiness in the younger man's pale face, so close to fear, it made his chest ache. Abe frowned.

"I'll tell you later," Sonny said.

Abe nodded, looking away, wondering what had him so shaken.

"You know, I'm almost to the point of believing you like these little visits, Sonny," Nate drawled as he walked up the lawn.

"I-I don't. I didn't call you; the security company did."

Nate stopped at the bottom of the porch steps.

"Saw that," he said, eyes flicking back and forth between him and Abe. "What happened?"

"The security company said the motion sensor on the

north side of the house was triggered," Sonny answered.

"Did you see or hear anything?"

"No," he said. "I didn't."

"Did you see or hear anything?" He directed the question at Abe this time.

"No, nothing," Abe said. "We were locked in."

"Uh-huh," Nate said.

Abe felt Sonny tense at the skeptical tone in Nate's voice.

"We were. Abe got here, and I locked up behind him. And set the alarm."

"You seem awfully shaky this evening."

"I am. Someone was here and tripped my security system, and I can't help but think you still believe I'm somehow making all this up."

"Sonny," Abe said, trying to calm him down.

"It could've been a racoon, you know?"

Sonny shook his head, looking away.

"Nate."

"What? I'm just saying, he seems awful excited for any reason to direct suspicion away from him."

"Come on, I've been here the whole evening. Just like last time when I saw him lock the door behind him."

Nate looked incredulous. "Then what's your assessment, Officer Ellis?"

Abe squirmed a little at that. "It could've been a racoon or possum, sure. But after everything that's gone on around here, it's scary."

"You're right. It is. Especially with my best friend locked up in there." He fixed Sonny with a look.

Sonny crossed his arms over his chest. "This isn't me. I swear it. I wouldn't do any of this. Not to myself and certainly not to someone else."

Abe said, "Did you even check the street? The neighborhood? Just to see if anyone was acting suspicious? Or are your presumptions getting the better of you, Officer Landis?"

Nate's eyes narrowed at Abe. "Are you suggesting I'm not doing my job?"

"I'm suggesting that since the break-in, you've had a bug up your ass about this. I'm speaking with the captain tomorrow and asking that, from now on, someone else be sent out to deal with this if it continues."

"Oh, it will. He loves the attention too much."

"It's not me!"

"Enough! Make sure you add this to the file, please. You can go now."

Nate shrugged, turning to leave. "You gentlemen have a nice evening," he called over his shoulder as he stomped away.

* * *

Sonny let Abe lead him back inside. He fought the urge to squirm away from Abe's touch when Abe rested a hand on his back to guide him and reassure him.

Abe closed the doors, relocking them. "I don't know the code."

Sonny shook his head. "Forget it."

"Sonny…"

"What? For all the good it did."

"Come on, sit down."

Again, Sonny let himself be led to the couch, trying not to let his agitation get the better of him. But Abe must've been able to sense it, because he carefully sat on the coffee table in front of him.

"Talk to me. You were pale and shaky when you came outside."

Sonny looked over Abe's shoulder at the window, and Abe followed his gaze.

"That's the north side of the house."

Abe turned back to Sonny.

"I think someone was watching us." He leaned forward, running one hand through his hair, trying desperately to keep it all in.

"I think you might be right."

Sonny closed his eyes, fighting to keep his breath steady. *Don't break, don't break, don't break.* Abe leaned closer to Sonny but didn't touch him. Sonny remembered the hand on his shoulder and how he'd jerked away from it. *He doesn't know what to do, how to handle you when you're like this.*

"Tell me how to help."

"I don't know," Sonny said, half growling, half whining. He hated the sound of it in his own ears.

"No, not with this stuff. I don't know what to do about that yet. All I can say is that I believe you, and when I go in tomorrow, I'll make sure someone else is overseeing everything," Abe explained.

Sonny looked up at him.

"Tell me how to help you right now."

Sonny shrugged.

"I know you're frustrated, maybe even as upset as you were the other day," Abe said.

"I don't know. I'm sorry. I know I'm a monster when I'm like this."

"You're not a monster, not by a long shot. In fact, you kind of remind me of someone when you're upset."

Sonny peered up at him. "Who?"

"My brother, Rich. He'd get like that when he was upset too. And if you pushed too hard, forget it. He'd take your head off."

Sonny snickered, almost despite himself.

"Ah, is that the trick? Maybe just sprinkle in some jokes?"

Sonny wouldn't meet his eyes. "Maybe. I don't know. No one's been able to diffuse me before."

"You use these harsh words, *monster*, *diffuse*. You know you're just human, right? You're not a beast or a bomb."

"Sometimes I feel like I am. I don't try to be a hothead. I just get so frustrated when I feel helpless."

"You're scared, Sonny. And I think you're entitled to be. Not only are you being harassed, but the cops aren't being very helpful. You're in a new place" — Abe paused, shaking his head — "I get it. I'd be shaken up too."

Sonny nodded. "I'm like your brother. Is that weird?"

Abe softened into a smile. "You don't look like him at all. And maybe I'm wrong for making the comparison. But man, seeing you upset for the first time, it was uncanny. If you'd have thrown in a 'Fuck off, Abe,' I'd have been horrified."

Sonny frowned. "I wouldn't talk to you like that."

"And that's where you differ. Too many manners. Rich has never been a gentleman."

"Is he around?"

Abe fixed him with the arch of an eyebrow. "You mean to tell me no one has let it slip about my brother?"

Sonny smiled sheepishly. "Maybe once or twice. But I didn't want to assume what I hear through the grapevine is the gospel."

Abe nodded. "He's in Huntsville for armed robbery. He gets out next year, I think."

"I'd like to meet him. You know, assuming we're still close."

Abe studied him for a moment, reaching out to brush at his hair, touching his face. And this time, Sonny didn't jerk away or flinch. "There's my Sonny. *Always* the gentleman."

Sonny reached up and pressed Abe's hand to his cheek. "Would you, um, like me to reciprocate?"

Abe chuckled. "My balls might be as blue as my eyes, but I don't think either of us is in the right headspace to pick up where we left off tonight."

Sonny sighed. "I think you're right. I'm sorry, though."

"Don't be. Next time," Abe said, low and tender. "And there will be a next time."

He could feel Abe pulling away, could feel him leaving already. *I don't want to be alone in this house. Not tonight.* He leaned in and kissed Abe.

"Sonny…"

But Sonny didn't let up. He knew what he was doing and didn't care what it said about him. *For the first time since coming here, I don't want to be alone.* The thought circled in his mind, again and again. He reached for Abe, gathering him in his arms and pulling him closer.

"Sonny, wait," Abe said, his hand on Sonny's chest, creating distance between them despite Sonny's persistence.

Sonny looked down at him, desperate and embarrassed because of it.

"Talk to me," Abe said softly. "What's going on in there?"

Sonny shook his head, trying to dispel his own desperation. "Nothing. I'm sorry." His grip on Abe loosened.

Abe searched his eyes. "You know, one day, you're going to have to let me in. There can't always be the option of slamming that wall down when something's eating at you."

Sonny wanted to be irritated. He wanted to turn into the bear that couldn't deal with his emotions, like he had so many times after coming home. But, in the space of just a few weeks, maybe even just a few hours, Abe had dismantled that piece of him. The question was, did he resent it, or was he grateful?

Abe leaned in, nuzzling his cheek. "Please let me help you."

A lump rose in Sonny's throat. *This is why we fight so hard against it all.* Because there was absolutely no middle ground between stoicism and meltdown. "I don't know how."

Abe must've heard the roughness in his voice because his hold tightened a fraction. "You could start by asking me to stay with you tonight. Because despite who you are and how strong you are, you're a little scared."

Sonny sucked in a sharp breath.

"It's okay to admit that, you know? I'd be scared. Hell, I am scared." Tentatively, he pulled back enough to look Sonny in the eyes again.

"I am scared," he admitted, even if it felt like he was dragging every word out of himself.

Abe smoothed his hair back, and again, to Sonny's surprise, the gentle touches calmed and soothed him. "It doesn't make you weak to admit that. Or to accept comfort. You know that, right?"

"It feels weak sometimes," he said, leaning into Abe's touch.

"And that's okay. So long as you know it's valid, but not true."

Sonny swallowed thickly. "Will you stay tonight?"

Abe smiled. "Of course."

* * *

Abe was surprised when Sonny led him up to his room. The first thing he saw was the poster pinned to the wall above his bed.

Sonny stopped when Abe did, following his gaze to the poster. "Oh, it's just…"

"You're a True North fan, huh?"

Sonny flushed. "I am. Obviously."

Abe leaned against the doorframe as Sonny pulled out some extra clothes for him to sleep in. "Are you a James guy or a Kieran guy?"

Sonny looked over at him, then up at the poster. "Well, I really admire James…"

"But?"

"But come on, Kieran's a babe."

Abe chuckled. "I'd have to agree."

Sonny laughed. "Really?"

"Yeah, really. Us pretty guys can like each other too, you know."

Sonny shook his head, handing him the clothes. "These might be a little big on you."

"I could just wear my T-shirt and shorts. Unless that's too much for your delicate sensibilities."

"Suit yourself," Sonny said, seemingly unable to keep the smile from his lips.

They lay side by side in Sonny's bed. Abe wanted to slide over to him and lay his head on Sonny's shoulder, maybe snuggle against the side of his chest.

Well, truthfully, he wanted to be naked and recently satisfied in his arms, teasing him more about his musical tastes and listening to him try to defend them.

Okay, he wanted Sonny on top of him, in him, pushing him deep into the mattress with the force of his thrusts while Abe begged for more.

Instead, he lay a proper ten inches away from Sonny, like a perfect gentleman.

Many more thoughts like that one and you can kiss the whole gentleman facade goodbye. He squirmed a little, making sure all evidence that his thoughts were anything but mundane and pure was effectively concealed.

Sonny rolled onto his side, facing Abe. "Thank you," he said.

Abe mirrored his position. "Anytime," he replied softly. "I mean it."

They talked for a while like that, murmuring in the dark until sleepy voices gave way to even breathing and light snores.

Abe snapped awake at the groans behind him. At some point during the night, he'd turned, and Sonny had scooted closer until they were practically spooning. He barely had time to register what was happening before the groaning turned into wailing and then all-out screaming. Abe sat up, moving to shake him awake.

"Sonny, wake up."

Sonny shot upright, pushing himself off the bed and onto the floor, scrambling away from whatever had been happening in his dream.

"Sonny, hey, hey." Abe moved to come to him, but Sonny shrank back against the wall, arms up as if shielding himself.

Up and out of bed, the cool air hit him, and Abe felt the wetness on his shorts. "What the hell?"

Sonny's arms lowered slowly, and he looked around, seeming to finally grasp that he was home and not wherever he'd been in the dream.

Abe noticed the large wet spot at the front of Sonny's shorts and realized what had happened. "Sonny, you with me?"

Sonny looked up at him, confused, then embarrassed, then, noticing the wet on himself and Abe, ashamed.

"I-I'm sorry," he said, trying to compose himself when Abe could clearly see that he was anything but.

"Sonny, it's okay. It was a nightmare."

"I'm so sorry." He leaned against the wall to stand, visibly shaking.

"Don't be. It was an accident, that's all. Come on, let's get cleaned up." He made the mistake of touching him, and Sonny flinched away.

"Don't!"

Abe jerked away as if he'd been burned.

* * *

Mortified, Sonny turned into the bathroom and shut the door behind him. He stripped, enduring a level of shame he hadn't felt since he'd woken up strapped down to the bed in the psychiatric ward back home. His body ached with it as he kicked off the damp clothes. He'd sweated straight through his tank top. And his shorts, well...

He turned on the shower, as hot as he could stand it, and stepped in.

Please, just leave, he thought, hoping Abe would be gone when he got out. *This is why you're single, Sonny boy. Because this shit in your head is too deep to make someone else wade through it with you.*

He stood under the hot spray, hearing faint rustling in the bedroom. He then heard the washer start up downstairs. He wanted to cry then, even more than before.

I don't deserve it. He remembered his nightmare, which wasn't really a nightmare. Nightmares were bad dreams, things that didn't actually happen in real life, things that the daylight chased away for you with ease. No, that was a flashback, as real and vivid as it had been when he'd lived it. He heard a knock at the door and startled. The door opened a crack.

"Sonny? I can take your clothes and put them in the wash too," Abe said. Like it was nothing. Like he hadn't just...

Sonny's face burned.

"Sonny?" Abe prompted.

"By the toilet."

* * *

Abe sat on the edge of the stripped bed in his jeans, his button-down open, waiting for Sonny as he emerged. Though he was wrapped in a towel from the waist down, sex couldn't be further from Abe's mind. Sonny looked sullen and ashamed, his face a splotchy red. Abe reached for him.

"Don't," Sonny said.

"Now's when you need it, Sonny," he reasoned.

"Stop being so nice. I peed on you, for fuck's sake."

"So? I'm a cop. You think I haven't had worse thrown at me?"

The joke fell flat.

Sonny went to the dresser and pulled out fresh nightclothes.

Abe looked away as he dressed.

Once covered, Sonny sat down beside him. "Thank you for starting the washer," he said, his voice small, pained.

"Of course," Abe said, nudging his shoulder.

"I'm so sorry," Sonny said.

"Don't apologize."

"It's so fucking embarrassing," he admitted.

"Sonny, I'm not stupid. You're a veteran, and you said you did one tour overseas. I can see in your eyes that you've been through some shit. At least you're getting help for it now."

Sonny nodded once before stopping, his gaze hardening. "I never told you that."

Abe realized his misstep. "I meant it as-as a question. It's the logical thing, right?" But it was too late.

Sonny searched his face, then looked away, closing his eyes. "The police report."

"Sonny…"

"From Maryland. That's why Nate thinks it's me." He took a deep breath, and Abe felt the chill coming off him. "How long have you known?"

Abe swallowed hard, unable to come up with a rational explanation for not telling Sonny the truth.

"Right, the whole time. Got it."

"Sonny, please."

"Just in case there is any doubt about my 'violent tendencies,' the time I hit my mother, she startled me awake. It was an accident. I-I'd never hurt anyone. And I certainly wouldn't fake harassment like this."

"Sonny, I know you wouldn't —"

"Get out."

Abe looked at him in disbelief. "I've been on your side this whole time. I believe you!"

"Just not enough to be honest with me?"

Abe felt sick. "You're not listening —"

"I said get out!"

Abe felt Sonny's shout lodge in his throat, felt his eyes sting as he shoved his shoes on, and left.

Ten

Sonny lay curled into a tight ball on the bare bed. His accident hadn't seeped through to the mattress, for which he was grateful. He didn't have the energy to put on new sheets and covers, so he lay there, his legs folded up to his chest, his arms crossed around himself. He felt raw and exposed. Not only was he certain that someone had been watching them as he let his guard down to be intimate with Abe, but Abe had been lying about what he knew. The entire time they'd known each other, he'd known about the suicide attempt, the psychiatric stay, the "history of violence."

"I'm not violent," he whispered to himself. "It was an accident." But he knew how flimsy that sounded on the paper of a police report, no doubt bracketed by quotation marks and words like allegedly.

And yet, he got close to you anyway. He likes you, Sonny.

How can I trust that? He ground his teeth against his rising emotions. *How can I trust him?* The pain flared deeply, and he shivered against it, pulling his limbs tighter to himself.

He dozed off and on like that, waking because he was cold, slipping back to sleep because, well, what else was there?

The following morning, he forced himself up. He got cleaned up again, still feeling soiled even though he'd showered the night before, then made his bed. He picked up around the house, put in the dryer the sheets and covers Abe had thrown in the washer. That was when he discovered Abe's T-shirt and shorts mixed in with the covers and his own nightclothes. Guilt and embarrassment washed over him, feelings he shoved aside as best he could.

After that, he called the security company to inquire about having cameras installed. It was a steep upgrade, but they said they'd be in touch about it shortly. Just as he hung up with them, his phone began ringing. A Maryland phone number lit the screen, and he picked it up out of curiosity.

"Hello?"

"Sonny?"

Dr. Ford.

"Oh. Uh, hi."

"Yeah, uh-hi is right."

Sonny sat down at the kitchen table. "I've been meaning to touch base with you."

"Uh-huh," she said skeptically. "I don't understand. You were doing so well attending therapy here."

He sighed, rubbing his brow. "I know. It's just been strange, getting adjusted here in this new place."

"I understand, but therapy was supposed to help with that too."

"I know. I'm sorry, I…" He trailed off. *Because how crazy am I going to sound spilling my guts to her right now?* "I'm just sorry."

"I'd ask if you don't like your new therapist, but she says she hasn't even seen you yet."

"I-I've just been busy. Honest. Moving in and getting a car and a job, it's been a lot."

"Sonny," she said reproachfully. It made him think of his mother, of Maddy.

"You're right. I'm sorry, Dr. Ford. Truly," he said. "I'll do better."

"I hope so. And you know you can still call and leave a message or email me anytime. Just because you're down there doesn't mean I've abandoned you."

He bit his lip at that. "I know. Thank you."

"All right, I expect you to start attending therapy. Okay?"

"Okay," Sonny agreed. "I promise."

"Okay. Other than that, you sound well. How's Texas?"

Sonny sat in the waiting room of the therapist's office, thankful there'd been an opening on such short notice so he wouldn't be able to change his mind, and at the same time nervous as ever. It'd been so easy with Dr. Ford. His only hope was that it would be easy with this doctor too.

Because clearly, I can't do this on my own.

"Mr. Lakes?"

Sonny looked up at the blonde woman standing in the doorway. He approached her, hand out.

"Sonny," he said.

She shook with him, smiling warmly. "Dr. Carmichael. Follow me." She led him back to her office, which was different than Dr. Ford's back home. For one thing, it wasn't contained within a hospital. This was just a regular therapist's office in a small building that housed other medical practices. "It's a pleasure to finally meet you," she said without any chastisement.

"I want to apologize for being a no-show. I'd make

the regular excuses about moving, but I guess I was just nervous."

"You had a good rapport with Dr. Ford from what I gather talking to her," she said. "It can definitely be nerve-racking, trying another therapist after having that with a previous one."

He nodded.

"Well, as I said, my name is Dr. Carmichael. I've lived in Texas my whole life. I've known Dr. Ford for some time professionally and admire her work and her ability to connect with her patients. You're definitely not the first person I've encountered who was apprehensive about switching from her."

"You've had other patients come from Maryland to Texas?"

She nodded. "Other military, as well. Which is where I'd like to begin, if that's all right with you."

He sighed. "Sure. I was an army medic. I trained at Fort Sam Houston, which is where I sort of fell in love with Texas. I did one tour in Afghanistan, had a bad experience, and got shipped back here. I was honorably discharged shortly thereafter." She studied him, and he suppressed his irritation at that.

"That's quite the summary."

He shrugged. "That's what happened."

"Your file says you attempted suicide, that you have moderate to severe PTSD, depression, anxiety —"

"If you know, then why ask me?"

She folded her hands in her lap. "Because I want to hear your story, not study your file."

"Can't Dr. Ford tell you?"

"Sonny, I want to help you. I understand how hard it must be to open up; that I can gather from your file." She

116

paused, looking at him. "And your body language."

He looked down at himself, his arms crossed over his chest, his shoulders hunched slightly.

"Why are you afraid of telling me what happened?"

He shrugged again. "I don't know."

"Are you afraid I'll lock you up again? I know that stay in the psychiatric ward must've frightened you."

"I wasn't scared."

"Then tell me what you were."

"I just don't want anyone to know. I don't want to talk about it. I want it gone from my mind."

"I wish we could do that for you, but we can't. And really, I don't think you want that."

"Don't. You have no idea what you're talking about, saying things like that."

"Then explain it to me."

He placed his hands on his knees, steadying himself, taking a few deep breaths.

"Take your time."

"I was working in the infirmary. Aside from the occasional outburst or emergency, our base was pretty quiet. I mostly dealt with some idiot who ate something weird or cut himself working." He took another deep breath. "But then, one day, I was sitting there, and all of a sudden all these vehicles pull up outside and they haul in these two guys covered in blood, and—" He paused, making himself loosen his grip on his knees. "It was just me and a couple of female officers. It was lunchtime." He felt himself shaking, felt the sweat popping out on his face and neck. "One of them, he was my friend. Well, they both were, you got to know most people on base with you. But this guy, h-he was my buddy. We'd, um, h-he, we'd go out drinking or just, he'd s-stop by the infirmary just to, um…"

"Sonny," Dr. Carmichael interrupted him. He looked up at her. "Deep breath." He took one with her, the tension in him easing slightly. "Can I ask what your friend's name was?"

"Mat," he managed through trembling lips before continuing on with the story. "Th-there was this bomb, I guess, and they got pretty tore up. And I, I would've been fine I think, maybe, if it hadn't been my friend. I was trying to help any way I could, but he was practically in two and begging me to help him. And I c-couldn't. I couldn't help him." He leaned forward, shaking, running his hands through his hair. "I couldn't help."

Dr. Carmichael stood. "Sonny, may I give you a hug?"

He couldn't answer for the tears, but he nodded.

She approached him, sitting down next to him on the couch, and put her arms around his shoulders. "You have no idea how much I appreciate your service, Sonny."

It was an awkward side-hug, but Sonny accepted it because he felt like he was drowning.

"You were so brave, and I promise you, I'm going to do everything I can to help you." She pulled back, patting his back gently.

When he looked up at her, he was surprised to find tears welled in her eyes.

She sniffed. "Sorry."

"Don't be. Th-thank you, Dr. Carmichael."

She straightened herself, returning to her chair across from him. "Is that what you see when you have a flashback or nightmare?"

He plucked a tissue from the box on the coffee table between them, wiping his eyes and nose. "It is. Although, sometimes it's embellished to be worse or more drawn out."

"That's fairly normal for that sort of trauma."

"I just can't" — he stopped, shaking his head — "I just can't get past it. I do what I'm supposed to, what all the articles and books say to do."

"What do you do to take care of yourself?"

"I get up every day and do things. I work, I maintain my house. I try to make friends and socialize. I've been vegan since I came back from over there, so I'm pretty sure I'm eating healthier than I ever have. I try to get enough sleep, although it's hard sometimes with the nightmares."

"These are all good things, but what do you do for Sonny?"

He frowned. "I thought those things were for me."

She smiled. "What do you do to enjoy yourself?"

He thought about it. "I mean, I enjoy most of those things."

"What do you do just for fun? Just to make yourself happy?"

He shrugged. "I guess... I don't know. I have been seeing this guy, although that's not going so well at the moment."

She nodded. "Dating is good. What's not going well about it?"

He sighed. "He's a cop. And he knew more about my past than he told me." She looked confused, and he realized she had no context for that. He hadn't even told Dr. Ford or his family what had been going on in Sweetshade since he got there. "I've, um, been harassed by someone. I don't know who, but they spray-painted my garage, broke into my house, set off my security alarm, all different days."

"That sounds stressful and scary. You're seeing the investigating officer?"

"No." *God no.* He shuddered. "The guy I'm seeing is on the same police force, but he's not the one investigating the case. He and the investigating officer are friends, and he knew about what happened in Maryland. But he didn't tell me."

"That's a shame. Honesty seems very important to you, as it should be."

"I just hate that feeling that someone might be watching me, waiting for me to snap."

"And you think he was?"

Sonny thought back over their time together. Did it ever really feel like Abe was watching him? "Not like waiting for me to snap exactly. But sometimes…I don't know. I just assume people don't know what to do with me when I'm stressed. I barely know what to do with me."

"You've been through something that very few people have ever experienced. I'm your therapist, and I can't imagine what it's been like for you. People are curious, maybe even nervous around someone with PTSD until they understand it."

He closed his eyes, feeling the pain flare at the back of his throat, in his chest. "I know that. I just wish he'd been honest with me. I wouldn't have been mad. I know certain things come up when you're looking into something like this."

"Maybe you could try talking to him. It doesn't sound like there was any ill intent or malice in what he did. And it certainly sounds like you're still interested in him."

He met her eyes. "I am. He's nice to me. I don't feel so alone when he's around. The first time I got really upset around him, when the break-in happened, I sort of snapped at him for trying to comfort me. Not-not violently or anything. I just flinched when he tried to touch me, and I know I was prickly when we spoke. But after someone tripped the alarm and I got agitated again, it's like he already knew how to modify his actions to help me calm down."

She smiled warmly at that. "How did that feel?"

"Amazing. In all the time I've been back, no one's gotten it that quickly."

"What did he do differently that time?"

"He didn't touch me right away. I don't know what that's about, being so irritated when people touch me when I'm upset, but I can't stand it. He didn't need me to explain it."

"He probably felt bad when you flinched the first time."

Sonny nodded, feeling guilty about it. "I don't mean to."

"I know you don't. I'm not blaming you for the reaction or telling you it's wrong."

"He just, he talked to me, got me to smile. He broke the tension in me, and I can't even pinpoint how he managed it."

"Maybe he's been around someone with PTSD before?"

"Maybe," he said.

"Here's what I'd like you to do before our next visit. I want you to think of three things you can do for yourself just for your enjoyment. Not things you think you should be doing, but things you enjoy just because. And I want you to think about reaching out to this man you've been seeing…?"

"Abe."

"Think about reaching out to Abe and giving him a chance to explain himself. Because it sounds to me like he's good for you."

"Okay." He stood up, extending a hand to her. "Thank you."

She took it, shaking with him. "Thank you, Sonny. It's been a pleasure to meet and talk to you."

* * *

Abe walked out of the captain's office, satisfied with himself. Nate would be taken off Sonny's case. He and Nate were at odds over it, but Abe didn't care. It was absolutely unfair that someone so biased would remain the investigating officer.

"What if it's actually him doing it?"

"I was with him last night, the whole time," Abe said.

Nate rolled his eyes. "And that could've been a racoon that set it off; you don't know."

"You don't know him—"

"And you're too close to know him. Excuse me for not being swayed by a pair of pretty blue eyes."

Abe turned to Nate, eyes intense. "You're out of line, Officer Landis. You're not on the case anymore, and neither am I."

"Am I out of line, Officer Ellis?"

"Yeah, you are. He is clearly being harassed, and it was your job to investigate it, regardless of what you thought may or may not be going on."

"He's a veteran with severe PTSD and a violent

past."

Abe approached him, anger burning in his eyes. "That violent past you're hung up on? He says it was an accident. His mother woke him up from a nightmare, and he didn't know where he was."

"Yeah? And what if it's you next?"

Abe thought of how Sonny had scrambled from the bed, frightened and completely in another time and place, how embarrassed he'd been when he'd seen what he'd done in the throes of his nightmare. He thought of how he'd told him to get out once he realized how much Abe knew and hadn't been honest about, how violated he must've felt. "Don't worry, there won't be a next time with me."

"Oh yeah?"

"Yeah." Abe turned away, grabbing his keys, smartphone, and sunglasses from his desk.

"Abe…"

"I'll be around," he tossed over his shoulder, storming out before Nate could piss him off further. He stopped on the front steps of the police station, seeing that he had a couple of text messages from Sonny.

Hey. I'm sorry for lashing out last night.

Abe swallowed hard, biting his lip as he read the second message.

Can we talk?

He began typing a response, typing and erasing half a dozen times before giving up and calling him.

"Hey," Sonny answered on the first ring.

"Sonny," Abe said, sitting down on the steps, his legs shaky under him. "I'm so glad you texted."

"I just, I want to talk. I have some things to explain about my past, in my words, if you'd like to hear it."

"You don't have to explain anything to me," Abe said, hearing the guilty quality in Sonny's voice. "I should've been honest with you from the start. I'm the one who owes an explanation."

"Maybe we both do," Sonny said. "After I'm off tonight?"

"I'll meet you at your place."

"I can text you when I'm off. Should be around nine thirty."

"Sounds good."

"All right, I'll see you then."

"Okay. And, Sonny?"

"Hmm?"

"Thank you. Thanks for not throwing this or me away."

"I'll talk to you tonight."

They hung up.

Eleven

Sonny worked his shift at Tom's, trying to keep from watching the clock. He ran their conversation over and over in his mind, along with what Dr. Carmichael had said.

It's time to come clean. At least to him.

He tried not to get his hopes up, knowing that with such a rocky start, things may not pan out with Abe. But that didn't mean they couldn't try. It also didn't mean they couldn't be friends, even if it didn't work out.

"You seem pensive," Jean remarked.

He looked up at her. "Sorry."

"Don't be. I heard what happened, what Abe did, getting Nate off the case. Honestly, I think it's for the best."

"Me too. I just wish I knew what I did to deserve what he thinks of me."

"Nate's one of those people, like a dog with a bone." She smiled ruefully. "I promise he's a nice guy."

"Maybe if he likes you."

She leaned back against the counter. "You like Abe?"

Sonny met her eyes, trying and as always failing to keep the smile off his face.

"My, look at that sunny smile." She winked, and he chuckled.

"Stop."

"Is that how you got your nickname?"

"No. My dad's name was Sully for Sullivan. They named me Harrison and, well…"

"Sully and Sonny." She smirked. "Sounds like something out of a book."

"And yes," Sonny said. "I do like him. Abe, I mean."

"Good. He needs someone to tether him to the ground."

He searched her eyes.

"Not that I'd know," she said.

"What you don't know, you seem to be able to glean just fine, Miss Jean." He tried to drawl, cringing at himself.

"Ew, no." She laughed, shaking her head. "Never do that again."

He snorted. "All right, I won't. But I meant what I said."

"So did I. I know you will, but, be good to him."

He sobered. "Of course."

She smiled. "All right, get out of here. You've been watching the clock since you got in."

* * *

Abe pulled up to Sonny's house just in time to hear his smartphone ping.

On my way.

Abe sent back a smiley face and a thumbs-up emoji, then tucked his phone back into his jacket pocket. He sat in the car for a moment, letting the Queen song finish playing on the radio before shutting the car off.

"I blame you, Sonny," he muttered to himself with a smile.

Unable to make himself stay in the car with his

nervous energy, he got out, locked it behind him, and walked up to Sonny's porch. He stopped long enough to consider the alarm system, and noticed that the motion sensor light on the porch hadn't come on as he approached. He looked up at it, observing that it had been knocked loose, seemingly with force. In fact, it was hanging by a few wires and nothing more.

"What the fuck?" Abe climbed the front steps, bracing for the alarm to sound…but it didn't. He had time for the hair to stand up on his arms and the back of his neck before the first blow landed.

* * *

He'd just knocked the motion sensor loose when he heard a vehicle coming up the street. He crouched low on the dark porch.

"Fuck," he swore under his breath, then saw who it was.

Not Lakes. Ellis. He grimaced. What the fuck was he doing here alone? He wondered if Lakes had given Ellis a key and the alarm code. Ellis got out of his car and approached the porch, giving no indication that he thought he wasn't alone.

He watched Ellis notice the motion sensor, felt his careful footsteps as he ascended the porch steps, heard him swear. Ellis was facing away, studying the motion sensor, when he rose up, less than five feet away from him.

So much for cops' instincts.

He swung the baseball bat, catching him across the back, listening to the breath rush out of him as Ellis went to his knees.

He didn't stop there. He didn't stop for a while.

* * *

Sonny pulled up beside Abe's car in his driveway. He peered over and saw he wasn't sitting inside. It was a nice, warm summer night, so he figured Abe was likely waiting on the porch. He'd know to be careful of the alarm sensors.

He climbed out of his truck and jogged up to the porch. Only he didn't see Abe anywhere.

"Abe?"

He climbed the steps and nearly tripped over something. He caught himself on the railing and saw Abe lying on his back on the porch.

"Abe?" He scrambled to him, leaning over him. It was too dark to see well, but what he could make out stunned him. The whole upper left side of Abe's face was dark with blood that had begun to run into the roots of his hair.

"Abel?" Sonny touched his throat, feeling for a pulse. He was still searching, his hands shaking with adrenaline, when Abe seemed to become aware of him. He grabbed for Sonny, and Sonny cried out with fright.

"Ssh-shh…" Abe tried to speak as he reached for Sonny.

"No no, don't, don't try to talk," Sonny said. Finally, his training kicked in. He pulled out his smartphone and dialed 911.

"Nine-one-one, what is your emergency?"

"M-my name is Harrison Lakes, and I'm at 195 Third Street in Sweetshade. My friend, he's been hit or beaten or something. He's hurt and bleeding and we need an ambulance." He said it all, trying to remain calm and keep his voice clear, knowing all too well how important that was.

"Is he breathing?"

128

"He is, but he has some kind of head trauma. I'm not sure what happened; I just got here. I f-found him like this." Sonny cradled the phone between his shoulder and cheek, trying to get a better look at Abe. Just as he was becoming aware of how bad off he was, Abe began to violently shudder and shake. "He's having a seizure. Please, please hurry!"

The phone slid from his shoulder as Sonny carefully turned him on his side and held him tight as the seizure wracked his body.

"Come on, Abe, come on, just hold on," he said, his voice trembling.

By the time the ambulance arrived, he'd stopped convulsing. Sonny kept his fingers at Abe's throat, monitoring his pulse and breath. He was weak and fading, but Sonny kept talking to him. Over and over, words of encouragement, words of tenderness, anything to help keep him alive long enough for the ambulance to come.

Once it came, everything was a blur to Sonny. Someone pried him away from Abe as they stabilized him for movement, loading him into the ambulance. Someone asked if he was hurt himself. He looked down and realized his hands were covered in Abe's blood, smears on his arms and chest.

"No," he'd said. He wasn't hurt. But then he thought they might take Abe, might leave him there to wait and worry. *"Can I come?"* he'd asked. He'd been ready to beg, but it hadn't been necessary. They'd let him without question. It wasn't until later, when he saw himself in a mirror, that he knew they'd seen the shock in his face.

He climbed into the ambulance and sat to Abe's

right, taking his hand into his. That's when he really saw how bad Abe was. On the left side of his face, his eye socket and brow were obviously shattered, the skin over them marred and bleeding. If there was any eye left, there'd be no saving it.

Sonny felt his hand move and nearly jumped, looking down at it. Abe's right hand flexed, squeezing Sonny's. Sonny looked back up at his face and saw the remaining eye looking at him. His lips moved, but it was obvious he couldn't speak. Sonny wasn't sure if it was shock or brain damage. Or both.

He leaned down. "You're all right, Abe. You're gonna be all right, but don't try to talk now, okay?"

Abe seemed to understand because his lips stopped moving. Sonny squeezed his hand, cupping it firmly between his palms. He could see pain etched in what was left of Abe's face. He could see fear too. And for a moment, his face wavered, and Sonny saw the face of another blond. He closed his eyes tight.

It's not him. It's Abe, and you're in Sweetshade, Texas. Abe needs you, Sonny. That's his hand in yours, and he's not begging you to save him. You got to him in time, and he's got a good chance because of it.

When he opened his eyes again, he saw that Abe's eye had a dazed, faraway look. Sonny turned to the EMTs.

"We gave him a sedative and a mild pain reliever, just until we get him to the hospital and can figure out exactly what's wrong," one of them explained.

Sonny nodded, looking back to Abe. He held on to his hand with his right, and with his left he reached into the neckline of his T-shirt and pulled out the pendant he wore around his neck. A small silver cross on a thin but sturdy chain. He held the cross in his left fist, leaned his forehead against it, closed his eyes, and began to pray.

It felt like forever and no time at all before they were at the hospital. They rushed Abe inside on the gurney. Sonny followed as long as he could, knowing they weren't going to let him go far. Abe was in too bad of shape to be in an area that allowed visitors.

A couple of hospital staffers stopped him at a set of double doors they took Abe through.

"Sir, we can't let you go with him," one of the nurses said.

He nodded, feeling the strain inside, the lump in his throat, the cold sweat at his temples and palms. She touched his shoulder gently.

"Come on, this way," she said, guiding him to a small, dingy waiting area. "The bathroom is just over there if you'd like to clean up."

The suggestion sounded odd until he remembered the blood on him. *Abe's blood.* Suddenly, a fresh cold sweat broke out everywhere, and he rushed into the men's room, thankful it was a single-stall. He fell to his knees, heaving the contents of his stomach into the toilet, feeling the chills racing through him.

"It's just shock," he muttered to himself as he reached for the toilet paper and tore off a piece to wipe his mouth. "He's your friend and he's hurt." He let out a shaky breath, trying to steady himself.

After flushing the toilet, he stood slowly, leaning against the wall for support as he took several deep breaths. The nausea gradually subsided, and he regained the confidence to move. He walked over to the sink and saw himself for the first time since finding Abe. Dried blood all over his hands and forearms, on his shirt too. But it was the small streak on his cheek that got to him.

Sonny, please, the voice echoed in his mind. *Please help me, please!*

Sonny closed his eyes tight. There'd been more blood that day. So much more, all over him. He remembered it rinsing off him in the shower, coloring the water a dull pink as it circled the drain between his feet.

"It's not then," he said to himself. "It's now. It's now and maybe..." He trailed off, shaking his head, too afraid to speak it. He held his hands under the faucet, and it came on automatically. He rinsed as much blood off him as he could, avoiding watching how it colored the water, then soaped up. He took a sheet of paper towel and wet it, wiping the blood from his cheek. *How did I get it on my face?* Had he smeared it there himself while trying to help? Had it been from one of the times Abe reached for him? He had time to wonder if he'd just wiped away the last touch he'd ever feel from Abe, when a hard knocking at the door startled him from his thoughts.

"One second!" he called out, drying his hands and throwing away the paper towels before emerging from the bathroom.

He was immediately grabbed and slammed face-first into the wall beside the door.

"Harrison Lakes, you're under arrest for assault and battery," came words spoken in a familiar male voice.

"What? No! No, I didn't—" His words were cut off by the *snap* and *click* of handcuffs being placed around his wrists.

"You have the right to remain silent. Anything you say can and will be used against you. You have the right to an attorney. If you cannot afford one, one will be appointed to you."

"Nate, this wasn't me," he pleaded, knowing it was no use. He didn't fight, even though everything inside him screamed for him to.

"Do you understand your rights?"

"Yes," he said, thankful he'd already been sick. Because if he hadn't, he'd most certainly be now.

"Good. And it's Officer Landis, psychopath." With that, Nate, along with another officer, led him out to the police car and shoved him in the back.

During the ride, Sonny said nothing. He knew better. Since he'd come to Sweetshade, Nate had done nothing but twist his words and believe his actions to be less than savory. It was no use trying to reason with him.

* * *

Three days and several emergency surgeries and procedures later, Abe woke up. He opened his eye and was surprised to see Jean sitting next to him instead of Sonny.

"Sonny." He murmured it, almost absently.

Jean looked up from her smartphone.

"Abe? You waking up?"

He lifted his hand to his face, confused about why he couldn't see out of both eyes, and felt a bandage covering the upper left half of his face directly over his eye.

"No no, don't touch it," she said softly, getting up and gently pulling his hand away from his face.

"What happened to me?" he croaked, realizing how horribly dry his mouth and throat were.

"You don't remember?"

He cringed, trying to think. But his recent memories

were muddy, blurry.

"What happened? And where's Sonny?"

Jean looked apprehensive at that, and his stomach dropped.

"Where is he? Is he hurt too?"

She shook her head. "No, he's fine."

"Then where is he? H-he was here. He rode with me in the ambulance." He heard the desperation in his voice and didn't care.

She must've heard the rising panic in his voice too because she reached for his hand. "Abe, you have to stay calm."

"Then answer me!"

"He's fine. He's just fine, I promise."

"Then where—"

Nate came in then, carrying two cups of coffee.

"Where's Sonny?" he asked Nate.

But Nate wouldn't meet his eyes. "You need to rest."

Realizing he wasn't going to get any answers, he found his bed remote and pressed the Call button.

"Abe..." Jean began.

"No! Someone's going to talk to me, and sure as shit isn't going to be you two, apparently."

"Don't you care about what happened to you?" Nate asked.

"I know what happened. Someone beat the hell out of me, and Sonny saved my fuckin' life." He pushed the button repeatedly.

Jean looked to Nate pleadingly.

"If he's hurt too, I need to know! I-I didn't think he was, he was in the ambulance with me, but no one was looking at him, so—"

"Mr. Ellis?" a voice came through the bed remote.

"Yes, I'd like to see my nurse, please."

"Yes, sir," the voice responded.

"He's fine, Abe," Nate said, clearly irritated.

"Then where is he? Is he laid up too?"

Nate sighed. "He's in County."

Abe's jaw dropped. "Are you nuts?"

"The EMTs said he was covered in your blood when they came for you."

"He fucking found me! Someone beat the shit out of me with a ball bat, and clearly" — he motioned to the side of his face — "I was in pretty bad shape."

"You need to calm down," Nate said with an edge.

"He wasn't even at the house yet, you moron! His truck wasn't there because he was still at work with her!" Abe jabbed a finger in Jean's direction.

"EMTs also said he was eerily quiet, stoic almost, when he rode in the ambulance."

"You've got to be —" Abe took a deep breath, trying to keep his voice down. "He has PTSD. He was probably holding on to his composure with both fucking hands."

"Or he beat the hell out of you, and you're too fucking ignorant to see it."

"Nate," Jean began but was abruptly cut off.

"No. He's in County because he was at the scene of the crime and is the only person we can trace back there besides you. He was covered in your blood and acting strange when they picked you both up."

Abe took another deep breath, trying to clear the red from the edges of his vision. "And I'm telling you it wasn't him. He saved my fucking life by showing up when he did. I mean, for fuck's sake, Nate, I saw his headlights when he pulled up, and thanked God for it."

"He's right. Sonny was at work with me until nine

fifteen. He didn't have time to do this," Jean said.

Nate's jaw clenched.

"He texted me right around then to say he was on his way. We planned to meet at his house to talk when he was off work. You can check my goddamned call records and texts if you want."

"If you remember all this so well, then who did it, Abe? Who beat your face in and left you to bleed out on *his* porch?"

"I don't know. He came at me from behind. I couldn't exactly get a good look at him. But it wasn't Sonny and you know it. You know it doesn't fit."

Nate huffed, crossing his arms.

"Get him out of County," Abe practically growled.

"I'd like to wait for the fingerprints from the motion sensor to come back."

"Now!"

"All right, everyone out," the nurse said, finally showing up. "Mr. Ellis, we need you calm. You're still healing."

Abe looked over her shoulder, meeting Nate's eyes before he exited the room. "I'm fucking serious. I will call the captain from here if I have to."

Twelve

For three days, Sonny sat in a cell in the Nueces County Jail. Aside from being involuntarily held in the psychiatric ward after his suicide attempt, it was the only other time he'd been forcibly held anywhere. He hadn't had to share a cell with anyone due to the "violent nature of his crime," but it was only a small consolation. No one would tell him if Abe was okay, if he was dying or dead, nothing.

They'd taken his cross when they booked him, but it hadn't stopped him from praying. He hadn't truly prayed since before Afghanistan. He'd continued to attend church and go through the motions of his faith, but after what happened and how he'd fallen into despair, he hadn't been sure God was on his side anymore.

But God wasn't the only one he spoke to during those three days. He prayed to his father, even if it sounded crazy or stupid. He couldn't help it. Hell, he'd even prayed to Mat. Anyone he thought might be listening, he prayed to, and not for himself.

For Abe.

And finally, three days later, he heard keys in the cell door. He looked up to see an officer opening the door.

"Mr. Lakes, you're free to go."

Sonny thought for sure he was dreaming. There was no way Nate or anyone would let him go free. He hadn't hurt Abe, but he knew what Nate thought. He knew how it looked, how he'd looked.

"Come on, son."

Sonny stood up from the bed and followed the officer out, too shocked to say much except, "Why?"

"Officer Ellis came to. Raised hell, from the sound of it. Says you didn't do it," he explained, leading him out to the front of the facility. His necklace and other personal effects were returned to him.

"So he's okay?"

"Pretty banged up and lost an eye, but if he's well enough to put the fear of God into Landis and the others, I'd say he's probably okay and getting better as we speak," the officer said with a chuckle.

Sonny smiled, even as the tears stung the backs of his eyes. He wasn't sure who to thank, but as he left the building, he said a quiet thank-you to each of the three he'd prayed to over the past three days.

He took a cab home so he could wash up before heading to the hospital, and had to make himself walk up to his porch. He avoided looking at the spot where he'd found Abe, knowing if he saw the bloody patch, either his stomach wound turn or he'd discover a whole new set of images added to his PTSD reel. Or both. He wanted to be strong and well when he went to see Abe.

He let himself inside, quickly showering and changing clothes before heading right back out.

Abe was sitting up in the bed, flipping through TV channels, when Sonny came in. Same Abe, same longish blond hair and medium build. But, as Sonny approached him from the left, Abe didn't notice him at first. A stark white bandage covered the upper left half of his face, his hair sweeping across it.

"Abe?" Sonny said, not wanting to startle him.

Abe turned, lips parting, eye fixing on him. "Sonny."

"Hey," Sonny said, coming around to his right side. He sat in the chair next to the bed. "How're you feeling?"

"Fine. Well, maybe not fine. Lost the eye," he said, attempting to sound flippant about it. Sonny could hear the choked, slightly broken quality in his voice.

"I heard. I'm sorry I wasn't here when you woke up."

"Don't," Abe said. "If the nurse hadn't yelled at me about getting too excited, I'd have wrung Nate's neck for throwing you in County like that."

"It w-wasn't me. I swear it."

Abe reached for his hand, squeezing it firmly in his. "I know that. There's no way."

"Thank you."

"No, thank you," Abe said, again fighting the emotional edge in his voice.

"Abe…"

"I know you saved me." He pushed his hair to the side slowly, attempting to turn on the charm. "The nurses told me this handsome, sweet army medic kept me safe until the ambulance came."

Sonny chuckled, even as tears welled in his eyes again.

"Don't you start. I'm having a hard enough time," Abe said, smiling through his own tears. "Come here," he said, lifting his arms.

Sonny rose to sit on the edge of Abe's hospital bed, wrapping his arms gently around him, careful to not jar him too much. He breathed him in, kissing the good side of his forehead fiercely.

"S-Sonny," Abe whispered, holding him with both arms wrapped around his middle, his face buried against his chest.

Sonny felt him tremble, heard him sniffle. He closed his eyes and just held him, so thankful. "It's okay," he whispered, his voice shaking.

Abe pulled back and looked up at him. "I can't imagine how scary that was for you," he said. "You were so brave."

Sonny avoided Abe's gaze. "I'm not so sure about that."

"I don't remember the attack, but I remember when your headlights hit the house and porch. I remember you holding me, moving me when…" He trailed off. "I've never seen anything like it."

"I just wanted to help."

"And you did," Abe whispered. "I don't think I'd be here otherwise, no matter what you may think."

Sonny blinked against the tears. "But you are. That's all that matters."

* * *

Abe watched him sobering, watched the protective wall come down. *He's not going to accept that he helped. He doesn't believe it.* But that was fine. He'd convince him later, when he could be alone with him and really get him to listen. And he'd thank him every way he knew how.

"I'm sorry about Nate."

Sonny smiled, blue eyes sparkling then. "I heard you gave him hell when you woke up."

"You're not mad at all, are you? About being held?"

"Abe, I—" He shook his head. "You have no idea how bad off you were. And they hauled me off and wouldn't tell me if you were okay or not."

Abe studied him. "You really don't think about yourself much, do you?"

"Not when someone I care about might be dead or dying and no one will tell me anything."

Abe smirked. "You care about me, huh?"

Sonny's gaze met his, and though he fought his smile, Abe could see it in his eyes. "I might be beat to hell mentally and emotionally, but I am capable of caring."

Abe reached up, touching his cheek. "Well, I'm beat to hell physically, and that still made me nauseous, it was so sweet."

"I almost brought you flowers," Sonny said, pressing his hand over Abe's, turning to kiss his palm.

Abe fake-gagged. "Gross. Why didn't you?"

"For one thing, I don't know what kinds of flowers you like. For another thing, in case Nate was up here, I kinda thought he'd think I was laying it on thick."

"Fuck him," Abe swore with a sigh. "Cheating me out of flowers."

Sonny shrugged. "There'll be other times."

Abe bit his lip. "Because of you." He cupped Sonny's face between his hands then, making him look at him. "You know that, right?"

Sonny chewed the inside of his lip. "I can't help but think this is my fault. If I hadn't come here…"

Abe leaned forward and pressed his lips to Sonny's, stopping the thought before he could finish it. "It's not your fault," he said softly, kissing him again.

Sonny returned the kiss, clearly holding back.

"I'm going to allow these chaste kisses for now," Abe murmured against his lips, feeling Sonny's smile. "But when they let me out of here and I'm better, you're going to kiss me like a man."

Sonny nipped at his bottom lip. "I'm going to do a lot more than that when you're healed."

Hearing the warm promise in Sonny's voice, Abe felt his insides heat. "Do that again."

Sonny nipped again, eliciting a growl from Abe. "You're ridiculous."

"And you're turning me on," Abe said, leaning back against the pillows. "Cut it out."

Sonny shook his head with a laugh. Abe noted the flush in his cheeks, the sparkle in his eyes, and knew — this was his partner. Even if Sonny hadn't figured it out yet.

"By the way, it's roses," Abe said.

Sonny frowned, looking confused.

"My favorite flower. Yellow roses." He felt the heat in his cheeks and wondered if Sonny would think that was weird or stupid.

Instead, Sonny reached out and carefully swept Abe's hair back from his forehead, eyeing the blond strands. "I'll remember that."

* * *

Nate and Jean showed up just in time to catch Sonny and Abe lingering close, talking and smiling despite the circumstances. Nate cleared his throat as he stood in the doorway.

Seeing who it was, Sonny returned to the chair next to Abe's bed.

"I owe you an apology," Nate said to Sonny as he and Jean entered the room.

Sonny recoiled, not wanting to even look at him the wrong way. It'd been proven time and again that he

142

couldn't really trust him.

Nate came to stand beside him, holding out his hand. "I'm sorry, Sonny."

Sonny looked up at him, then his hand, then back at him before reluctantly taking it and shaking with him. "I wouldn't do this. Not to myself" — he looked over at Abe, bandaged and bruised, then back to Nate — "and definitely not to anyone else. I don't know how to make you believe me."

"Leave him alone, Nate," Abe said.

"No, I mean it. I'm sorry. They dusted that motion sensor for prints and couldn't find any to match Sonny's. They did find some, which I thought might be from the tech who installed them, but he happened to be in the system from a while back. They weren't his."

Surprised, Sonny asked, "Who was it, then? Did you find —"

Nate shook his head. "None in the system. We found the same prints on your side door, and if I had to guess, we'd find them in your house too, from the break-in."

Sonny swallowed, relieved and horrified in the same instant.

"I am sorry. Truly. And if you decide you want to pursue legal action, I wouldn't blame you."

"I don't."

"Sonny —" Abe began, but Sonny cut him off with a look.

"I don't." He looked around at them, feeling their eyes on him. "I just want it to stop."

"Then I think your best bet is to have that motion sensor replaced, along with adding cameras. I know your guard has to be up already, but make sure you're alert and aware when you're home. Especially when you're coming or going," Nate explained, clearly desperate for Sonny and Abe to forgive him.

Sonny nodded.

"We could arrange a patrol car to circle more frequently, couldn't we?"

"You say *we* like you're going to be back anytime soon," Nate ribbed him. "You've got some healing to do first."

"I could stay with you," Abe said to Sonny.

Sonny looked up at him, startled. "Absolutely not. You've already been seriously hurt once at my place."

"I'm going to need help while I recover, Sonny. The brain damage is minimal, thank God, but it's not nothing. And after the prosthetic surgery, I'm going to need help adjusting."

Sonny looked to Nate. "He's in no shape to try and protect me or intervene if something were to happen."

"Don't talk about me like I'm not here," Abe snapped.

Nate put his hands up. "Maybe it's not the worst idea. The EMTs said you were pretty savvy with the medical stuff. And Abe—brain-damaged or not—is a good cop."

Jean touched Sonny's shoulder. "Just think about it, Sonny."

They released Abe into Sonny's care after all, and Sonny accepted it without protest. The nurses showed him how to clean and dress the wounds on Abe's face, even though he already knew what he was doing. He would just be doing it under less pressure than if he were on the job.

Abe squirmed and flushed the first time Sonny saw

his face bare, but Sonny didn't waver. The nurse walked him through it as he cleaned and redressed it with a firm, gentle touch and a steady, calm demeanor. He'd watched Abe relax, watched it sink in that he wasn't going to turn green with disgust or cringe in horror at the sight of him. Neither of them spoke about it during, nor after. They didn't have to.

"All right, can he walk?"

"There's nothing wrong with my legs," Abe said with an edge.

The nurse sighed, having dealt with him off and on for the past week. "Stay close to him. If anything seems off, make him sit down."

Sonny carried Abe's bag, filled with paperwork, extra bandages, and antibiotic cream, his hand hovering behind Abe's back as they walked.

"I can feel you watching me," Abe muttered in the elevator.

"This'll go a lot smoother if you just let me fuss over you," Sonny retorted.

Abe looked up at him, narrowing his eye playfully. "Are you my caregiver or my warden?"

"I'm whatever I have to be to get you better."

Abe nudged him. "You're cute when you're serious."

Sonny shook his head, chuckling.

He drove them back to his house. In the days Abe had been in the hospital, he'd cleaned up the porch and had the motion sensor fixed, along with the installation of security cameras.

By the time he got Abe inside, it was clear that the sass on the way out of the hospital was just because he was ready to be out. Sonny watched him sit down, watched as he leaned back, huffing a sigh of relief. He sat down on the edge of the coffee table in front of him and touched his face.

"Tired?"

Abe nodded. "Very."

* * *

Abe watched Sonny carry his things in and set the security system once they were inside. He watched him sit in front of him, and wanted to be irritated when he touched him, clearly out of worry rather than affection. But seeing those clear blue eyes gauging and measuring him, knowing he was checking for anything amiss in his face or the temperature of his skin, he just couldn't be. Because it *was* out of affection.

"Do I look okay?"

Sonny nodded. "Just tired."

The sweet concern in his voice caught in Abe's throat.

"You know, all bullshit about not letting me be home alone aside, I'm glad they let me come home with you. That *you* let me come home with you. I guess we didn't really get to talk, about before."

Sonny shrugged it off, moving to stand. "Don't worry about that now."

But Abe grabbed his hand. "I do worry about it."

Sonny sat down beside him. "We can talk about it when you're rested. But I promise, I'm not upset anymore."

"I can take it if you are, you know? I'm strong enough that if you're still angry, you don't have to suppress it."

Sonny held his hand, looking down at it. "The only thing that upset me was the possibility that you thought I was so unhinged, you couldn't be honest with me."

146

Abe winced. "I never thought you were unhinged. But, out of context, the thing with your mom did worry me."

Sonny nodded, his eyes sad. "I know. Believe me, even in context, I'm still ashamed."

"You couldn't help it, Sonny."

Sonny blinked, and Abe watched him shove his emotions down. "I've gone back to therapy. I stopped when I moved here, but I'm back at it now."

"That's good," Abe said. "I'm glad for that. For you."

"Maybe when we're not so worn out, I'll tell you about it."

"You don't have to tell me anything you don't want to—"

Suddenly, Sonny was kissing him. "I know I don't. But I want to."

Abe nodded, cupping his cheeks, leaning in to kiss him again.

Later that evening, after dinner and dozing on the couch together, Sonny led Abe upstairs. Abe showered, careful of his face, then let Sonny do his magic. He watched Sonny as he removed the bandage and studied the wounded area.

"B-bad?"

"Not at all. It's healing up great."

"No, I mean..." Abe paused, nervous. "How bad do I look?"

"You look like a guy who's been beaten, but you don't look bad. They did a great job of stabilizing and reconstructing the socket," Sonny said as he cleaned the open spots.

"You think so?"

Sonny smiled at that, eyes meeting his briefly before returning to the task.

"Look, jerk, I know I'm cute. I just want to know if I'm still going to be cute when I'm healed and the prosthetic is in."

Sonny took some of the antibiotic cream and, gentle as ever, applied it to his face. "Yes, dear, you're going to be as cute as ever."

"You think I'm cute?" He winked and then realized how weird that must've looked.

Sonny snorted.

"Ha-ha. You try flirting with a busted face," Abe said.

"Hold still," Sonny said as he took a new bandage and pressed it carefully, one side after another, over the affected area. After making sure the bandage was placed properly, he turned to the sink to wash his hands.

"You didn't answer my question, Dr. Lakes," Abe said.

"You know I think you're cute," he said, drying his hands. "You're flirting with me through what I know has to be at least some pain." He held out his hand, and Abe stood with him. Abe wrapped his arms loosely around Sonny's waist, closing his eyes as Sonny kissed his forehead.

"It's not so bad," Abe said, breathing him in. "Just a dull ache most of the time."

Sonny held him for a moment before leading him out to the bedroom.

"You can sleep here; the sheets and everything are clean," Sonny said, grabbing one pillow and the throw blanket at the end of the bed.

Abe frowned. "Where are you going?"

"I'm sleeping downstairs on the couch."

"Uh-uh, you're sleeping next to me."

Sonny shook his head. "That's not a good idea right now."

"I'm not saying come on to me or anything, but—"

"No, I mean"—Sonny's jaw tensed—"it's not...safe."

"What do you mean, not safe?"

"Abe, you've seen me come out of a nightmare. I'm not here, I'm not aware of anything or anyone around me," Sonny explained. "I can't risk hurting you."

And just like that, Abe understood. *He's afraid of waking up like that and clocking you in the face. And right now, who knows what kind of damage that could do.*

"I'm sorry. I swear I'm not trying to be dramatic or standoffish. But I won't risk it," he said quietly, shame coloring his cheeks.

Abe swallowed, looking around. "I understand. But you should let me sleep on the couch, then."

"Absolutely not. You're healing. You need good rest."

"You're also cute when you try to be bossy."

Sonny shook his head, fighting a small smile tugging at his lips. "I'll be downstairs. Just call my phone or come get me if you need me."

Abe nodded. "Okay."

Thirteen

Sonny settled in on the couch, thankful he'd gone with a nice, plush option. He placed his smartphone—ringer turned all the way up—on the coffee table and leaned back against his pillow.

Abe was safe and healing, upstairs in his bed.

He thought about the wounds, about finding him hurt and bleeding, and continued to be shocked at his own strength during all of it. Six months, even a year ago, he'd have been too shaken to help or care for him. At the worst moments, his mind had tried to play tricks on him, to make him see Mat instead of Abe.

But Abe wasn't Mat. Aside from the blond hair and light eyes, they were nothing alike. Abe might be a cop, but there were distinct differences between law enforcement and military. Abe was also older, snappier, and less naive than Mat. But Mat had been a good man, all the same. Sonny chewed his lip. They'd been close but never crossed the line. Even after the repeal of Don't Ask Don't Tell, you weren't exactly open and out in the military. At least, they hadn't been. Still, after everything, if Mat had made it, he'd have pursued him.

"Stop, Sonny," he muttered to himself, knowing he was playing with fire, thinking of all of it so late at night. He rolled onto his side, facing the back of the couch, and crossed his arms. He closed his eyes and waited for sleep.

* * *

The next morning, Abe crept downstairs to find Sonny still curled up on the couch. He approached, then thought better of it. Even if he didn't wake with a start, he'd be irked that Abe took the chance. Instead, he sat on the arm of the couch by Sonny's feet.

How much has he stressed? he wondered. *How little sleep – good sleep – has he had?* He'd badly wanted Sonny to sleep next to him, wanted to be able to roll over and find him there, warm and solid, and snuggle close to him. He respected Sonny's wishes, but it didn't mean he didn't still want it. Him.

He reached out, touching one calf. "Sonny?" He shook him gently until he woke. Not with a start or with ghosts in his eyes. Just adorably sleepy and momentarily disoriented.

"Shit. What time is it?"

"Eight. I'm sorry, I know that's early, but…"

Sonny sat up, rubbing his eyes with the heels of his palms. "No, I'm sorry. I should've set an alarm. How's your head?"

"Achy but okay," Abe said. Little tufts of dark hair stood up in the back and to one side of Sonny's head, the side on which he'd been sleeping. Unsurprisingly, the tousle endeared him to Abe even more.

"All right, come on. Let's go look at your head, get some pain meds in you," Sonny said, coming alert best he could.

"Don't rush," Abe said, reaching out to smooth down his hair.

Sonny looked up at him, lines from the pillow pressed into his cheek.

"You slept hard," Abe said.

"Must've," he said, pushing himself up. "Come on."

He followed Abe upstairs and tended to his wounds again, giving him the pain meds, noting down the time and dose.

After they'd taken care of that and Sonny started coffee and breakfast, Abe broke it to him.

"So, uh, don't panic, but my folks want to see me."

Sonny nodded. "Okay."

"Okay?"

Sonny flipped a couple of eggs in a separate pan from his tofu scramble before turning to face Abe. "Yeah, they're your parents."

"That's not weird?"

"That your parents would want to see you after you've been released from the hospital? No, Abe, it's not."

"They'd have to come here…"

Sonny brought their breakfast over to the table. Tofu scramble with veggies and hash browns for him. Eggs, bacon, and hash browns for Abe. "I know, unless you want me to take you to your place."

"You're really not fazed by meeting my parents?"

"Should I be?"

"It's just, the last time I introduced them to a guy I was seeing, it didn't exactly go well," Abe explained.

"I guess that would depend on how you introduce me."

"Ha-ha, nice try. They know I'm gay. And they're gonna see that you're handsome and taking care of me," Abe said.

"I can't tell if you're asking me to play your boyfriend or not."

Abe met his eyes across the table. "I don't want you to play anything."

Sonny wiped his mouth with his napkin. "Are you asking me to be your boyfriend, then?"

Boyfriend, Abe thought, looking at Sonny. *Isn't that what you want?*

Sonny added, "I hate to break it to you, but I kinda thought I already was."

"You are?"

Sonny smiled, eyes sparkling bright despite everything. "I mean, we've gone on a date..."

"Two."

"Ah, yes, two dates. We've kissed. We've done...other stuff. You're letting me look after you while you heal."

"Shit. I guess you are my boyfriend," Abe played along, trying to keep from completely beaming.

"If you want me to be," Sonny said, teasing tenderly.

Abe nodded, feeling himself blush. "How do you do that?"

Sonny took a bite of his scramble. "Do what?"

"You're so damn cute and unassuming, it's almost annoying."

Sonny bumped his knee against Abe's underneath the table. "If that blush is you being annoyed, then I'd love to continue to annoy you."

Abe smiled despite himself. "They want to stop by this afternoon. Is that okay?"

"Of course," Sonny said, stopping to take a drink of his coffee. "*Boyfriend.*"

* * *

Sonny dressed and made sure the house was in order and Abe squared away before Abe's parents showed up. Nervous though he was, defining their relationship over breakfast gave him new confidence.

He and Abe were sitting in the living room when they knocked at the door.

Sonny took a breath, smiling nervously at Abe.

"Don't worry," Abe said, releasing his hand.

"I'll try." He got up and opened the door. "Hi. You must be Mr. and Mrs. Ellis." He stepped aside, holding the door open. "Come in."

"Richard," the older man said, shaking his hand.

"Sonny." The first thing he noticed was how Abe seemed to be the perfect mix of his parents' features, although the blond-and-blue combination clearly came from his mother. The next thing he noticed was how Abe's mother brushed past him.

"Abel," she said, going to her son at once.

"Hey, Mom." He stood to hug her.

"Your face," she said, looking him over.

"I'm fine," he said when she cupped his face, examining the bandaged area. "Really. Sonny's been taking care of me."

She pursed her lips at that, and Sonny felt the tension in the room surge.

"We really appreciate that, Sonny," Richard said.

"He's an army medic," Abe said, laying it on thick.

"We saw the stain on the porch."

Sonny swallowed nervously, bracing for her to blame him.

"Mary, now, be nice," Richard said. "Army medic, you say?"

"Yes, sir. Well, former. I was discharged about a year

ago."

"Were you overseas?"

"One tour in Afghanistan," he said, hoping they wouldn't press further. They didn't. In fact, it seemed to give Mary pause. "Would you like anything to drink? I have coffee."

"I'd like a cup," Mary said. "Please."

Richard smiled, turning to Sonny. "I'll help you, son. Come on."

* * *

Abe watched his father soften toward Sonny and knew it was the military background, paired with the squeaky-clean appearance. Not that it was an act. It was all Sonny.

"Well, he's certainly an improvement over the last boy you introduced us to," Mary remarked.

"Gee, thanks, Mom," Abe said, sitting down with her.

"How are you, really?"

"It's achy at times, but Sonny's helping me keep a close watch on it. I'll have the prosthetic surgery as soon as my skull heals," he said, and watched her stifle a shudder.

"Sorry, I just can't imagine," she said. "What exactly happened? I mean, we heard, but…"

"Mom."

"I'm just asking, Abel. That was scary, that cop coming to the house in the middle of the night."

"I'm sure it was. But I'm fine."

Richard and Sonny returned with four cups of coffee.

"The boy's vegan, Mary. He had your almond milk creamer," Richard said with a smile.

Sonny handed her a cup.

"Thank you, Sonny."

"Of course." He sat down next to Abe.

"Thank you," Abe said, taking his cup from his father.

"So, Sonny, been in Sweetshade long?" she asked, peering at him over the cup.

"No, ma'am. Only about a month or so."

"And what brings you here?"

"Mom."

"It's okay," Sonny said. "I trained at Fort Sam Houston and kinda fell in love with Texas then. I'm from Maryland, and while I liked it there, I just love this perpetual summer."

Abe couldn't believe how Sonny did it, smiling and saying things like that, charming his folks. Not in equal measure at first, no. Mary clearly didn't trust him. But he was wonderful, even under his mother's scrutiny. By the end of the visit, both were charmed by him, and Abe found himself even further in it for Sonny than before.

* * *

Sonny closed the door behind them and had just enough time to turn before Abe had him pinned against the door, seizing his mouth in a kiss.

"How did you do that?"

Sonny chuckled, wrapping his arms around Abe. "Do what?"

Abe slipped his hands into the back pockets of Sonny's jeans.

"Hey now."

"You know what. You say a few things and smile and

draw people right in," Abe said, pulling him close, pressing kisses along his jaw, down his throat. "You were so charming, it turned me on."

"I was just being me," Sonny said.

Abe arched an eyebrow.

"Me on my best behavior," Sonny corrected with a smile.

"No, that was definitely you," Abe said, kissing him again. And again. "Take me upstairs," he murmured.

Sonny tensed. "I don't know if that's a good idea yet."

"We can go slow," he said, pressing his hips to Sonny's, and Sonny could feel how turned on they both were. "In fact, I want you to."

"Abel," Sonny said, apprehensive.

"Harrison," Abe countered. "You're not going to hurt me or break me, I promise."

Sonny swallowed nervously, and Abe seemed to see it then, that maybe it wasn't just Abe's current condition. Maybe he was just nervous, regardless of circumstance. Abe pulled back.

"Shit, I'm sorry. I'm not trying to…" He shook his head. "Fuck, I'm sorry." He pushed his hair back from his brow. "I'm such an asshole."

Sonny reached for him. "You're not. I want you too." He sighed. "I'm just nervous."

Abe narrowed his eye comically. "Oh, shut up. Just like everything else, you'll start doing it and knock my damned socks off."

Sonny smiled. "I don't know about that."

"I do," Abe said. "I've seen you. And I've watched and felt you when you let yourself have what you want."

Sonny flushed, remembering how Abe had dropped

to his knees, remembering how he'd encouraged Sonny to let go with him.

"How you can blush talking about it and then be so damn sexy in the moment is beyond me," Abe teased him.

"All right, come on," Sonny said. "But we're going to do it slowly, my way. And the second you start to feel off, I expect you to tell me."

Abe's face lit up, and he raised his hand, three fingers up. "Scout's honor."

Sonny laughed, shaking his head as he followed Abe upstairs.

* * *

They got to Sonny's bedroom, and Abe stopped, turning to him.

"Kiss me," he said, leaning in.

Sonny happily obliged, kissing him with a fevered tenderness that Abe was quite certain only Sonny could manage. His lips were soft, full without being a prominent feature, and Abe loved them, loved the way he kissed with them.

Sonny snaked an arm around him and walked him backward until the backs of Abe's legs touched the bed.

Abe reached for Sonny's shirt, pulling it loose and unbuttoning it. But Sonny didn't just stand there and wait. He ran his big hands up and down Abe's arms, kissing his mouth, his cheeks, his jaw, everywhere he could reach.

Abe had the shirt undone and pushed it down Sonny's broad shoulders. Sonny let the shirt drop before reaching for the hem of his T-shirt and pulling it up over his head, uncovering more and more to love about the man's body in addition to the man himself. Abe drank him in, his thick torso lined with muscle but still soft somehow. *Perfect.* Abe leaned forward to nuzzle his chest, pressing kisses against the smooth, flushed skin. He stopped at the small silver cross on a matching chain, long enough that it easily hid beneath his shirts. He touched it, holding it between his fingers, looking up at Sonny.

"Sorry if that's weird."

Abe pulled him back into a kiss. "You really do save kittens in your spare time, don't you?"

Sonny snickered, shaking his head. "No. Just scrappy little cops."

Abe chuckled. "Damn right."

Sonny reached down and pulled Abe's T-shirt up, careful not to disturb the injured side of his face. He tossed the shirt away, and suddenly Abe felt self-conscious. Sonny looked him over, seeing the bruises on the rest of his body. One long bruise across his upper chest and arms, and Abe knew he'd be shocked by the few across his back when he saw them.

"I didn't know there were more marks," Sonny said.

Abe crossed his arms, cupping his elbows. "I'm fine, Sonny."

Sonny must've heard the uncomfortable note in his voice because he met Abe's gaze once more. "I'm sorry. I just didn't know. Are there more?"

Abe sighed, turning around. He heard Sonny gasp under his breath, felt his touch at the edges of the different bruises.

"Abel…"

"I'm fine."

"Is anything else broken?"

"A couple of bruised ribs," he said, increasingly

exasperated. "Nothing I haven't had before."

"Abe…"

But he was grabbing for his shirt. "Never mind. Wouldn't want to risk setting off those alarm bells in your head if you whacked a bruise making love, right?" He felt Sonny recoil at the cheap shot.

"Look at me," Sonny said.

Abe turned slowly, trying to meet Sonny's gaze and failing.

"I care about you, and I don't want to hurt you worse," Sonny said, his voice firm. "It has nothing to do with my PTSD."

Abe felt stupid and ashamed for having said it. "I know. I just, I can't stand when you look at me like that."

To Abe's surprise, Sonny nodded in understanding. "I know the feeling. That look people give when they think you might fall apart."

"I might not be as big or as strong as you, but I'm still here," he said, swallowing against the emotion even he couldn't fathom. "Because of you."

Sonny softened at that.

"I'm sorry," Abe said. "That was a low blow, and—"

But Sonny was right there, taking the shirt from him and tossing it away once more. And his hands were everywhere again, sliding over Abe's body. Strong, broad fingers running through his chest hair, brushing his nipples. He rested his forehead against Abe's.

Abe shook his head. "I won't go there again. I promise."

Sonny's hands stopped at the top of Abe's jeans and began undoing them. He leaned in, his lips near Abe's ear. "Turn around."

Abe did as he was told, and Sonny pushed his pants

and underwear down, helping him step out of them. He rose slowly, kissing his way up Abe's legs, lips dragging and pressing on his calves, his thighs, hands smoothing and touching. "S-Sonny," he whispered when Sonny stopped short of touching him intimately.

"Get on the bed." Abe did so, crawling onto it, feeling Sonny's eyes on him. "On your back." Again, Abe obeyed, turning to lie naked on Sonny's bed.

Sonny undid his own pants, stepping out of them and his underwear before joining Abe.

How the man could look even bigger naked, Abe didn't know. Muscles bunched and released as he crawled onto the bed, thick and broad.

"Fuck, you're a sight," Abe said as Sonny settled between his legs.

"So are you," Sonny said, kissing his mouth once before trailing down his throat, nuzzling his chest, not seeming to mind the hair there as previous lovers had. He mouthed each nipple, then kissed lower and lower.

Sonny paused, rose back on his bent legs, looking Abe over.

"You look ready to pounce," Abe said.

"And you look good enough to eat," Sonny countered. "Hand me the lube. Bedside drawer."

Abe reached over, found the small tube, and gave it to him. But Sonny didn't open it yet. No, instead, he grazed the underside of Abe's cock with his palm, watching him squirm.

"You're so hard," Sonny remarked, more to himself than anything, as he bent forward and took the tip of Abe's cock into his mouth.

Abe watched him...and then, blissful sucking as Sonny drew back until it popped from between his lips.

Sonny did this a few more times, until Abe was panting, practically ready to beg, before he paused. "How's the head?"

"What?"

"Your head, how is it?"

Abe laughed breathlessly. "It's fine. No more than a dull ache."

Sonny smirked. "Good. Hand me a pillow."

Abe handed him one of the sham pillows, and Sonny carefully placed it beneath Abe's ass.

"Knees bent, legs apart."

"You know, these commands are almost as filthy as regular dirty talk," Abe commented, bending his knees and spreading his legs.

"I'm glad you think so," Sonny said, the color in his cheeks soaring. "I'm not much good at dirty talk."

"You don't have to be," Abe said.

Sonny chuckled, kneeling between his legs, wrapping his hand around Abe's cock once more. Only this time, he nuzzled beneath at his balls, sucking them, one at a time, into his hot mouth.

"Oh my God," Abe swore. Sonny worked back and forth a few times before Abe felt wet, obscene kisses against the backs of his thighs, the cheeks of his ass.

To Abe's frustration, he rose up once more.

"*What?*" he whined.

Sonny laughed. "Put your arms under your knees and pull your legs up."

Under Sonny's gaze, Abe felt heat bloom in his cheeks and chest as he obeyed. "L-like this?"

"Mm-hm," Sonny cooed, looking him over. "Just like that." He turned his attention back to Abe's body, kneeling into a comfortable position. His hands were on

162

Abe, stroking his cock and sac, pushing his ass and thighs open. His gaze was heavy and hot, and Abe felt something graze his hole, back and forth, making his breath hitch. "You are so damn gorgeous, Abel. On fire like this for me."

"Sonny, please," he moaned. "I want you so much."

Sonny leaned down, and suddenly those fleeting little touches were replaced with something warm and wet and so intimate, it made Abe's toes curl. Sonny's tongue traced a circle, around and around his hole, stopping occasionally to flick directly over it before returning to the lazy circles. Over and over and over.

"S-Sonny," Abe groaned, feeling sweat pop out on his chest and throat. Completely vulnerable and bare and spread open with Sonny kissing him, eating him. It was almost too much to bear.

"Relax for me," he murmured, teasing him once again with his thumb.

Abe tried to take a deep breath, but with the way Sonny was touching him, it was nearly impossible to control specific parts of his body. Sonny seemed satisfied, because after a moment he was back, his tongue not only circling and flicking, but pressing forward until it breached the tight ring of muscle. Abe gasped as he repeated the motion several times, until Abe's resistance was depleted. "You're killing me," he panted.

"You have the cutest little ass I ever saw," Sonny remarked, his voice warm and intoxicating as he let up, again kissing his thighs and cheeks, stopping once to nip at the undercurve of one ass cheek.

"Sonny, please, please," Abe begged.

Sonny lifted up on one arm, looking up at him. "Please what?" He teased Abe's hole with the pad of his thumb.

"Ooh, please, please fuck me." He wriggled back against the sensation, seeking more.

Sonny chuckled, picking up the lubricant again. "Shit, hang on." He went to the bathroom, coming back as quickly as he'd gone, condom in hand. "Like I said, I haven't done this in a while. I wasn't organized for it."

Abe laughed at that. "Sonny Lakes disorganized? I don't believe it."

"Ha-ha." He applied the condom to himself before uncapping the lube.

And suddenly there were fingers pressing into him, one, two, three, opening him slowly, carefully. Sonny turned them, and Abe gasped.

"Oh-*oh*," he moaned loudly as Sonny stroked his prostate. His cock jumped, lifting off his lower stomach a couple of times. "Fuck. Get down here."

Sonny withdrew his fingers and lined himself up against Abe's ass. He paused long enough that Abe looked up at him, pushing demandingly against Sonny's cock. "Slow. I mean it."

Abe nodded. "I promise. Just, please, put that thing in me before I lose my mind."

Sonny laughed, pressing inside.

Abe gasped, letting go of his legs, one hand at his cock, the other on his chest.

Sonny stopped about halfway and drew back before pressing forward again.

"F-fuck, you're big," Abe said, his ass gripping Sonny tight.

"Am I hurting you?"

Abe shook his head. "No, God no." His back arched as Sonny drew back, then pushed forward, this time until he was fully sheathed. "Oh fuck."

"You fit like a damn glove," Sonny bit out.

Abe's gaze focused on him, and he saw how much Sonny was holding back. All the strength and power in that big, broad frame, and he was getting maybe a third of it. He understood why, but in the future, when he was healed and well, he'd demand that Sonny let loose and really let him have it. He'd beg for it, even. After the glimpse of what it was like when Sonny let go before, he could only imagine what it would feel like. He reached for Sonny then. "Get this damned pillow out from under me. I want to hold on to you."

Sonny pulled the pillow out from under him, and suddenly they were much closer, the angle much more intimate. Abe wrapped his legs around Sonny's hips, his hands smoothing over Sonny's back and sides.

"Fuck," Sonny swore, humping and bucking into Abe, kissing him between feverish breaths.

"That's right. Fuck." Abe arched back against the bed, enduring the increasingly powerful, punctuating thrusts into his body. "Fuck me."

Sonny reached between them, stroking Abe's cock in opposite rhythm, creating a constant stream of pleasure. "You have no idea how much I've wanted you," Sonny panted. "How much you turn me on."

Abe could see the truth in his blue eyes, even amid the flushed cheeks and kiss-swollen lips. "I feel the same. The exact same," he said. He leaned in, kissing Sonny's throat and chest, sucking his nipples.

"Abe," he moaned, pushing just a little harder into him at the suckling.

"I'm so close," Abe said, arms around Sonny, fingers digging into his back.

"Come, come for me," Sonny encouraged.

Abe looked into his eyes, felt him, and lost it. He came hard, his seed spilling in bursts over Sonny's hand, over both of their torsos. "You too," Abe said, pushing back, matching his passion. Sonny frowned, then moaned at the increased friction and pressure.

"Abel," he panted, his thrusts gathering speed and power for a moment before Abe felt him lose it. "Oh f-fuck." His breath hitched in the middle of the swear as he spilled inside the condom.

Abe held him. *I've never seen anything so beautiful*, he marveled, watching Sonny come up close like that, watching him try to fight the hazy afterglow and keep his wits about him. "Slow, Sonny, slow," he said softly. "Take your time. Let it subside on its own." He brushed his fingers through Sonny's short, dark hair. "I'm just fine."

Sonny opened his eyes, fighting to focus.

Abe smiled up at him. "Damn. It really has been a while, hasn't it?"

Sonny chuckled breathlessly. "It has." He withdrew carefully, his limbs shaky.

"Easy, big guy," Abe said, helping him to his side. "I think you fucked both our brains out." Abe gently removed the condom and tied it off, then tossed it into the trash can under the bedside table. He looked back at Sonny, stretched out on his back, catching his breath, one arm tossed over his head, the other hand resting on his chest.

"I swear I'm not a virgin," Sonny said.

Abe lay down beside him, resting his chin against the side of Sonny's chest. "Of that much, I'm certain. I can't wait till I'm healed."

"Why?"

"Because I want to feel you at full strength."

Sonny laughed in earnest. "I can't wait either." He brushed Abe's hair back from his face. "How're you feeling?"

"Fine. Achy, but fine. You didn't make anything worse," Abe reassured him.

Sonny held him close, and Abe laid his cheek against Sonny's shoulder, settling against him. *This is my mate*, he thought as Sonny kissed the top of his head, his hands smoothing and kneading his bare skin. *This is him. My him.* He wrapped his arms around Sonny's middle and burrowed close, thrilled when Sonny held him just as firmly, hoping he felt the same.

* * *

He stalked up to the house as dusk settled around him. Lakes's truck was in the driveway next to Ellis's car. The fag cop had survived.

In all honesty, he hadn't meant to beat him so badly. He hadn't meant to beat him at all. He'd come to Lakes's house to wreak a little havoc. He hadn't anticipated Ellis showing up, much less being trapped on the porch when he did. And the little bastard had good instincts, but was too slow on the uptake. He could've beaten him to death if he'd wanted, easily. But then, like clockwork, he'd heard Lakes's truck approach. He'd taken off.

No more. Absolutely no more of that.

He walked around the house, just out of reach of the motion sensors and cameras, unable to spot either of them through the windows. Which was fine. They were probably upstairs, blowing each other.

He spat once before walking back to their vehicles.

Lakes's was the farthest away from the house and security measures.

He smashed the baseball bat through the windshield of the truck.

Fourteen

The distant smash of glass permeated Sonny's sleep. He didn't snap awake or anything too jerky with Abe curled at his side, his head on Sonny's shoulder as he slept. He wanted to be annoyed that Abe had let him doze off with him in the bed, but in the aftermath of their lovemaking, he couldn't find it in himself. He dismissed the noise as a fluke, settling back and pulling Abe tighter to him, kissing his hair, eyes falling closed as he relaxed. But then he heard another loud crash of glass. "Abel," he said, shaking Abe gently.

Abe came awake, looking around confused. "Shit, sorry."

"Shh," Sonny said, listening for more.

Another crash.

"What the..."

But Sonny was up, pulling his jeans on. "Stay here."

* * *

Abe pulled his clothes on, and for about two minutes, he obeyed Sonny's orders. But the longer Sonny was downstairs by himself, the bigger the pit in his stomach grew. "Fuck this." He left the room and took the stairs slowly, the growing dark not helping with his newly constricted vision.

Sonny stood in the living room, peering out the

window.

"Sonny?"

Sonny whirled, startled. "I told you to stay upstairs."

Abe heard the bite in his tone but didn't care. "What was that?" He saw the phone in Sonny's hand.

"I already called the police. It looks like someone broke my truck windows."

Abe approached slowly, sensing Sonny's agitation. "Did you see anyone?"

"No," Sonny said. "If I hadn't fallen asleep..."

"Hey," Abe said, touching his shoulder. He felt Sonny start to flinch and stop himself.

"I'm going to go get dressed," he said. "Please don't go out there."

* * *

Both of them were dressed by the time the police arrived. Nate was one of the officers who showed up.

"What are you—" Abe began.

"I asked for him and another officer," Sonny said. "He knew you were here. I figured he'd want to see you were okay."

Abe smiled at that, feeling the significance of that gesture.

"What happened?" Nate asked as he and another officer approached Sonny's front porch.

Sonny descended the steps to meet them. "I'm not sure. We didn't want to come outside until you guys showed up."

Nate and the other officer, Gonzalez, followed Sonny to the driveway. Shattered glass crunched under their shoes. Sure enough, someone had broken all the windows

169

on his truck.

"Shit," Nate remarked, observing the spray of glass shards littering the driveway.

"What's that?" Gonzalez asked, peering through the hole where the driver-side window had been.

Sonny looked in and saw it—an old, worn, wooden baseball bat. Goose bumps rose on his arms and neck when he noticed the dried blood at the broad end. He heard a gasp behind him and turned to see Abe, white as a sheet, gaze fixed on the bat.

"N-Nate, h-he was with me all evening. I swear," Abe stuttered.

"I know. I know, buddy," Nate said. "No one thinks it's him. I promise."

Sonny felt sick to his stomach. Abe, faced with the object used to nearly beat him to death—and which retained remnants of his beating—only thought to defend him.

"You said you heard glass breaking? How long ago?" Gonzalez asked Sonny.

"About twenty, twenty-five minutes ago. I was asleep, so I'm not sure if I heard everything or not," Sonny explained.

Abe made to lean against the truck and swayed. Sonny caught him.

"Let's go sit down," Sonny said, guiding him back to the porch. He'd intended for them to go inside, but Abe sat down on the steps.

"I don't feel so good," Abe said.

"What doesn't feel good?" Sonny asked.

Abe held his hands out, showing Sonny how they shook.

"Headache? Nausea? Keep talking, Abe," he

encouraged.

"No, not my head. Like a panic attack."

And just like that, Sonny understood what was happening. *Jesus, Sonny boy, took you that long? How many times have you seen blood or gore or anything remotely like that day and lost it?* He sat down next to him.

Nate and Officer Gonzalez finished taking their statements, and though Nate looked concerned for his friend, they left.

"Abe?"

"Get my gun," Abe said between deep breaths. "Glove box."

Sonny hated it, but he nodded. He stood, and using Abe's car key, retrieved the firearm.

"I'm sorry, but we have to keep it in the house," Abe said, taking it from him when he brought it back.

"I agree," Sonny said. "Come on, let's go inside." Abe took his extended hand, and Sonny felt the cold sweat on his palm as he led him into the house. He guided Abe to the couch and sat him down.

Abe placed the gun on the coffee table, hands continuing to shake as he did. "Fuck," he swore, running his hands through his hair.

"Tell me how to help," Sonny prompted.

"I don't know. I don't know what's happening to me."

"May I touch you?"

Abe looked over at him, confused at first, then nodded in understanding.

Sonny touched him, rubbing soft circles in the center of his back.

"D-did they take it away, you think? The bat?"

"They did. I saw it." Sonny watched tears threaten in

earnest then. "It's okay, Abe. It's okay to be upset or scared again."

Abe took a deep breath, fighting himself. "That's, that's the thing..." He trailed off, unable to finish the thought.

Sonny reached for him then, pulling him into his lap. Abe didn't fight. He curled against him, letting the tears come. "You're okay. I'm going to keep you safe." Abe leaned into his chest, quaking, and Sonny kissed his forehead, his hair, held him tightly. "I promise."

Sonny held him like that for a long time, rocking and cooing, vowing he would do everything in his power to keep his promise.

That Sunday, Sonny went to church. Abe didn't tease him for it, though he declined to join him.

"I won't begrudge you for it, but it's not for me," Abe said, clearly wondering if this was going to be a point of contention between them.

"I understand," Sonny said. "I'm not going to shove my beliefs down your throat."

Abe raised his eyebrows mischievously, and Sonny couldn't help but smile back.

"However you're about to twist what I just said, you can save it," he said with a chuckle.

"I was just going to ask if you planned to stop by the firehouse on your way home to see if any kittens need saving first," Abe quipped.

"You know, just for making that joke repeatedly, I'm going to bring a kitten home one day and you're going to help me take care of it."

"Ew, you're a cat person?"

Sonny laughed. "I take it you're not."

"Have a good time," Abe said, straightening his collar for him. "Say thanks to the guy upstairs for me. You know, just in case."

Sonny smiled, shaking his head as he left.

Sonny sat in a pew a few rows from the front. Ever since Abe had pulled through and they'd grown closer, Sonny felt he had a lot to thank God for.

He'd worn the silver cross around his neck for years. He'd received it as a gift from his parents on his eighteenth birthday as part birthday present, part congratulations/good-luck gift when he joined the army. He'd worn it up until he'd been deployed overseas, during which time he'd given it to his mother for safekeeping. Part of him wondered if that wasn't the reason his tour in Afghanistan had gone so badly.

Jo had promptly returned the cross to him when he came home, and he'd dutifully worn it. But it'd been all but for show. Sure, he'd gone to church after returning to the States, but after losing Mat, after the PTSD and depression sank their claws into him, he felt like God was angry with him. He never completely lost his faith, but he'd wondered for a while if God had lost faith in him. So he'd stopped talking, stopped asking for help, and wore the cross as a reminder of everything he felt he'd lost.

But then, in the grips of panic in the ambulance, as Abe lay beaten and bloody and nearly dying, he'd inexplicably reached for it. Holding Abe's hand in one hand and his cross in the other, he'd prayed for the first time in years.

No. He'd begged. He'd pleaded for God to hear him, to help him, to have mercy on Abe. Even if Sonny felt he didn't deserve his grace, maybe Abe did. He'd been quiet, too afraid to pray aloud. Not for fear of scrutiny, but for fear that God would think him too desperate. Or think that Sonny only prayed when he wanted something.

But somehow, it seemed that God had heard him, had deemed him worthy of his grace after all. Abe pulled through with minimal brain damage, and though he'd lost an eye, he hadn't lost anything else. He was the same Abe, shaken but still snappy and spry and as full of life as he'd been since Sonny had known him. No, he'd never drag Abe here, never preach at him or try to make him believe. But he could certainly try to show thanks to God for both of them.

So here he sat, in the pew of the Episcopal Church of Epiphany, in Sweetshade, Texas, thanking God for all of it. Reverend Charleston's words filtered in from time to time, comforting him with his reassurances and prayers.

After the service, Sonny rose to leave, but was stopped by a hand on his shoulder.

"Sonny," Reverend Charleston said warmly. "I'd figured you'd be tending to Officer Ellis for the next few weeks."

Sonny smiled. "I am. But he's doing well enough that I can still come."

Daniel smiled back. "Thanks for a few answered prayers?"

"Yes, actually."

"That's wonderful. I'm glad you came today. I have something for you. Well, for Officer Ellis."

Sonny watched as he pulled an envelope from his back pocket.

"A small collection for Officer Ellis's care. He and the Sweetshade Police do so much for all of us. I was hoping you'd be able to give this to him for us," he explained.

"Oh," Sonny said, taken aback. "Well, I can try, but I kind of think—"

"If he won't accept it for himself, tell him to give it to a charity of his choosing."

Sonny nodded. "Okay, I will. Thank you."

Just as he tucked it into his own back pocket, Mason approached them. Sonny caught his eye and watched him hesitate, felt the discomfort in him rise. *He's just a boy.* But something about Mason made him feel...off.

Daniel followed Sonny's gaze, and with that, Mason came the rest of the way to join them.

"Mason," Daniel said. "Everything okay?"

"Everything's fine," Mason replied.

Sonny felt the tension ramp up, and decided it was time for him to head home. "Well, thank you again. I can't promise Abe will take it, but—"

"Abe?" Mason asked.

No, Sonny thought. *Sneered.*

"Officer Ellis," Daniel said.

"Right, sorry. I can't promise Officer Ellis will accept this, but I'll see to it he does what you asked if not," Sonny said. He held out his hand to Daniel, they shook, and then he held out his hand to Mason.

Mason pointedly refused to shake Sonny's hand.

Back in the car—Abe's car, since Sonny's truck was in the shop having the windows replaced—Sonny shrugged off the uncomfortable encounter. He turned on some music to center himself as he drove to his place.

* * *

Abe was curled up on the couch, dozing to one of Sonny's records, when Sonny returned home.

175

Home? This isn't your home, Abe. But it'd begun to feel that way. Home, at Sonny's side. Slowly but surely, he'd let Abe closer to him. First by taking care of him, meeting his folks, claiming his *boyfriend* title. Then by making love, slowly and carefully for now while he healed. But God, it was everything. And then by holding him, sleeping in bed with him. To their surprise, Sonny's nightmares had all but ceased since Abe's attack.

He heard a car pull up in the driveway and stood, peering out to be sure. But of course, it was only Sonny coming back from church. Abe smiled at that. *If he were any more squeaky-clean, I'd have to wonder.*

"Hey," Sonny said, coming in and closing and locking the door behind him.

"Hey," Abe said, accepting the sweet hello kiss when it came. "How was it?"

"About like it is every week. Although, I do have something for you," he said, reaching into his back pocket and handing him an envelope.

Abe looked inside, seeing the check within. "What's this?"

"I guess they took up a collection for you after what happened. Reverend Charleston asked me to give it to you."

Abe shifted uncomfortably. "But I'm not a member of the church."

"Churches do that sometimes, regardless," Sonny said. "He said if you didn't want to take it for yourself, you could donate it."

Abe chewed his lip.

Sonny leaned down to kiss his temple on the good side. "It's just people being nice. Don't overthink it. Come on, let me make you some lunch."

Abe nodded, following him into the kitchen. He watched Sonny make them both sandwiches with raw veggies on the side. Sonny must've felt his gaze.

"I promise, I'm not going to slip you any fake cheese," Sonny said, the smile evident in his voice.

Abe walked over to him and wrapped his arms around Sonny's middle. "I know. You just take good care of me, is all," Abe said, kissing his neck once. Sonny shivered, patting Abe's hands where they met just above his stomach.

When everything was ready, they sat at the table and ate quietly for a few moments.

"So," Abe said, "I'm thinking they'll check my face at my next appointment and maybe schedule the implant in the next couple of weeks. If I'm healed enough."

"That's great, Abe."

"I'll need more help," he said, testing the waters. "Just until I get used to it and make sure it's right."

Sonny reached for his hand. "Abe—"

"I'm not overstaying my welcome, am I?"

Sonny frowned, incredulous. "Please."

"I'm serious."

"I don't mind you being here," Sonny said firmly. "At all."

"Really?"

"Really. It's been nice, having you right there when I wake up," Sonny said.

"When you want some action?" Abe winked, and Sonny chuckled.

"Maybe that too, but"—he squeezed Abe's hand—"not just that. You know that, right?"

Abe smiled, then frowned slightly. "You're too sweet for your own good."

"Been a long time since I cared about someone. Forgive me if I overdo it."

"Oh, you don't *overdo* anything. You just say things that make me want to crawl in your lap and beg you to *overdo* it, is all."

"I don't know what I do, but I guess I'm glad I do it."

"You guess, huh?"

Sonny smiled up at him.

"So," Abe said, sobering. "Would you mind taking me to the surgery when the time comes?"

"Not at all," Sonny said. "Mind if I fuss over you when it's all over?"

Abe groaned. "You know, you really should be a nurse or doctor." As soon as he said it, he wished he hadn't. Because once it was out, he had to watch Sonny retreat, had to watch the clouds dim the sparkle in his eyes. "Shit. I'm sorry."

"Don't be. I should. I just can't." He shrugged, picking up his mostly empty plate and tossing the leftovers into the trash.

"Sonny," Abe said, touching his arm. "Please don't shut me out."

"I'm not," he said. But he already had, hard.

And Abe almost let him get away with it. Almost.

"Sonny, stop," he said, following him into the living room.

Sonny stopped, and a beat passed before he turned back to Abe. "What?"

Abe felt it in his throat, his chest. A burning love battling with a frustrating, cold anger. "You do realize you saved my life, right? That you've nursed me back to health?"

"I got lucky!"

Abe hadn't expected him to shout, and he jumped, startled. Sonny went to turn away again, but Abe wouldn't let him. He charged over to him, took his arms, and held him still. "Stop running from me."

"If I wanted to run, I would."

"You're running now. Every time you do this, you're running. And I get it. I understand you've had some kind of trauma—"

"Then understand!"

"I am your partner! If you can't let me in, then wha—" He stopped, feeling the choking tears in his throat.

"I am letting you in," Sonny ground out.

Abe looked up at him, shaking his head. "Not really. We haven't even talked about why I was here that night."

"Because you were hurt!"

"I'm fine! I'm h-healing," he said, fighting the urge to cry.

"Fine. What do you want to know, huh?"

"Don't," Abe said. "Not like this."

"No, honestly, what do you want to know? I was a medic in Afghanistan, and I was too young to know it wasn't for me." He sat down on the couch, running his hands through his hair.

Abe sat next to him and laid a hand against his back. To his surprise, Sonny didn't jerk away from his touch.

"I was only there for one tour because, by the time it was done, I was such a mess, they couldn't risk anything but discharging me."

Abe leaned over and kissed Sonny's shoulder. "Keep talking."

"I l-let my best friend die."

"What was his name?"

"Mat." Sonny said it with a quiet sorrow that suggested they'd been more than friends. "I was all alone for the first time, so far away from home, and h-he—" Sonny stopped, fists clenched on his knees. "He was like me. Like us."

"You liked him?"

Sonny nodded, eyes closing tight, tears streaming down his cheeks. "Th-there was this roadside bomb, and he-he got hurt. Bad. They brought him back, and"—it began spilling out of him then—"Jesus, Abe, he was practically in two. I don't know how they got him back to base alive. And there was nothing I could do. Nothing."

Abe ran a hand over the back of his head, feeling sympathetic pain searing the inside of his own chest.

"He was bleeding, and there were just, pieces of him, hanging out. And he was begging me to help, screaming at me to help him."

Abe choked back tears, listening to the pain in Sonny's voice, the raw despair.

"By the time he died, his blood was all over me. Just, everywhere. I don't remember much right after. One of the other medics must've cleaned me up because I woke up a few hours later on a cot of my own." He wiped a hand over his face. "After that, I was useless at my job. I couldn't do anything without having flashbacks."

"It wasn't your fault," Abe said.

"I know. I just..." He shook his head. "He was my friend. It's bad enough to not be able to help a stranger. But when the guy dying on the table is pleading for you to help him by name?"

Abe reached for the tissues and offered them to him. Sonny took a couple and blew his nose.

"Anyway, it got so bad, they had to ship me home

180

and discharge me. Honorably. I still maintain my benefits and everything. But I was an absolute wreck. PTSD, depression, anxiety. You name it, I have or had it. Nightmares and flashbacks so bad... I mean, you saw what can happen. I was wound so tight after I accidentally hit my mom, I just nosedived."

Abe nodded, continuing to stroke his back in wide, soothing circles.

"That's why there's a record. I tried to kill myself, and they locked me up for a few days." He sniffed, wiping his eyes. "But it was for the best. I met there the first therapist who actually helped me. Got on medication." He seemed to remember he was talking to Abe and looked over at him.

"You were so calm and sure when I was hurt."

Sonny reached over, touching the good side of his face, leaning his forehead against Abe's. "I got another chance to get it right."

Abe swallowed hard, looking up into his bloodshot blue eyes, at his nose and cheeks, red and puffy from crying. "I love you. I'm so in love with you."

Sonny gasped.

"I'm sorry if that was the wrong moment. You don't have to say it back. But I do. I am."

Sonny chewed his lip. "I think I love you too."

"You think?" he asked with humor in his voice.

"I know."

Sonny reached over and lifted Abe into his lap, as he'd done the first time they were intimate with each other. Only this time, he wrapped his arms around Abe and held him tightly, his face buried against Abe's chest.

"Look at me," Abe said softly, holding him but trying to lean back.

Sonny looked up at him, smiling through his tears.

Abe cupped his face in his hands. "My sweet boy." Sonny leaned in again, rested his cheek against Abe's chest, and Abe held him, pressing kisses against his dark, silky hair. "My sweet Sonny," Abe cooed.

"I love you, Abe."

Abe heard the choked tears in his voice and held him all the tighter.

Fifteen

Back home, in the bathroom, he carefully unwrapped his hand. He knew he'd allowed his rage to get the better of him, let himself go so far, he'd not noticed getting cut on the breaking glass.

He was testing you. They both were. *He examined the exposed wound on his hand. Not too deep and probably not infected, but it still smarted and bled if he messed with it too much.*

Like I didn't know they were upstairs screwing each other. *He sneered as he poured rubbing alcohol into his palm, enduring the sting in silence.*

"Penance for such thoughts," he murmured to himself.

He'd walked around Sonny's house, careful no one saw him. Having seen no one but knowing both men were home, it was telling where they were and what they were likely doing.

He rinsed the alcohol away, letting the wound breathe for a moment before jamming his thumb into it and hissing in pain. "Penance for such thoughts."

A knock came at the bathroom door.

"Just a minute," he called out. He applied antibacterial cream, then rewrapped his hand and put everything away before coming out.

His father eyed him. "What happened to your hand?"

"Nothing. Just a scratch."

"From what?"

He smiled at his father, looking away.

"What's going on? You've been disappearing, then returning all worked up, with that look on your face."

"Just doing the Lord's work, Reverend Charleston," he said solemnly.

* * *

Daniel had begun to suspect that his son was harassing Sonny. He hadn't at first, not when it was just spray-painted profanities and one lone break-in. Sonny was new in town, and not only were people curious to a fault, but kids could be cruel. He was openly gay, and in a small town, even one as accepting as Sweetshade, there were always going to be people who didn't approve.

But then, as Officer Ellis got involved with Sonny, he noted a change in his son. Mason had always disliked the openly gay cop. Daniel didn't care that Abe was gay. He was a good cop, and Daniel felt lucky to have him around. But not Mason.

It was strange because his wife hadn't been this way. He didn't think she took much notice of anything that didn't have to do with him, Mason, or the church. Maybe she disapproved, but if so, she wasn't outspoken about it. Daniel's philosophy regarding his church and faith had always been a forgiving, accepting one. But after her death, Mason started taking everything in the scriptures as unyieldingly as possible. It was alarming how much his faith and worship had changed right before Daniel's eyes.

Since Sonny's arrival in Sweetshade, Mason had changed again. Daniel knew the moment Sonny said he was homosexual that Mason would react. He'd braced for it, hoping Sonny wouldn't think he felt the same as his son, that he'd recognize that Mason's beliefs and thoughts weren't a reflection of his own.

With all this swirling in his mind, Daniel waited for Mason to leave, then crept into his room.

It was surprisingly barren for a boy of nineteen. Orderly and neat, his bed made, and almost no clutter to speak of. Daniel studied his son's bookshelf, finding several Bibles, along with a few other books by religious-leaning authors. It made him sad, how little Mason was willing to step outside himself and his beliefs. No music, he didn't even have a stereo. No computer, no television. He knew all this, but confronted with the harsh reality, it was startling.

He retreated, closing the door behind him, shaking off chills. He still suspected, but found nothing that pointed directly to Mason as the person harassing Sonny.

* * *

Sonny returned to work the following week, finally comfortable enough to leave Abe alone for longer than an hour or so. Not that he worried about him in his house, but head trauma was strange and could present odd symptoms and issues without warning. Aside from a few headaches and mild confusion at times, Abe seemed normal.

Sonny was wiping down the bar and setting the glasses to his liking when Jean walked up.

"Hey there. How's he doing?"

"Good. Seems to think he's better than he might actually be."

She rolled her eyes playfully. "He's a handful. I wouldn't expect any less, even on the mend. How're you holding up?"

He looked over at her. "I assume Nate told you about the bat and my truck."

"He did."

"I just don't understand, and frankly, I'm scared. It was one thing when it was all aimed at me and relatively harmless. It's another when they beat the hell out of someone I care about."

"I'm so sorry, Sonny."

"I just, I saw enough violence when I was overseas, you know?"

She nodded. "Is he going to have the prosthetic implant soon?"

"As soon as they clear him for the procedure."

"Well, when you need off for that, let me know. We can cover for you."

"I really appreciate that," he said, scratching the back of his neck nervously. "You guys barely know me."

"Seeing you with him in the hospital," she said, touching his arm, "I know all I need to."

The next couple of weeks went by without incident, and Sonny cautiously hoped that things had finally settled down.

He and Abe coexisted in his house nearly seamlessly, eating together and living together and making love. To his surprise, his nightmares seemed to have all but ceased, and he'd begun to trust himself to sleep next to Abe at night.

Abe seemed to relish it, often curled at Sonny's side or spooned from behind. It felt amazing to have someone like this, so completely. It dawned on him that it was possible he was experiencing love for the very first time.

Real, honest, consuming love he hadn't even known he'd been craving. He'd experienced the first shivers of feelings for Mat, but this with Abe? This felt real and solid, and he leaned into it. Abe made him laugh, made him talk, made him so comfortable and assured that he felt himself really open up for the first time. Abe knew what Sonny perceived to be the worst things about himself and loved him anyway.

So, as he sat in the waiting room while Abe was having the prosthetic eye implanted, he felt nervous, anxious. The risk was very low, but he still worried.

"Mr. Lakes?"

Sonny looked up at the young nurse.

"Mr. Ellis is through and asking for you."

He beamed, coming to his feet at once.

She smiled at him. "This way."

"Did it go well?" he asked as he followed her.

"Very. I'll let you see for yourself." She pulled back the curtain to Abe's recovery room.

* * *

Abe sat there, nervous. He'd seen himself in the mirror and knew that aside from a few faint scars and a slightly too perfect prosthetic eye, he looked like himself again. But it wasn't just him now. He wanted to know what Sonny thought.

Not that he has it in him to sneer and turn away. Still, he wanted Sonny to see that he was healed and well. He wanted him to feel confident with him. All the held-back touches and careful lovemaking frustrated Abe, and he was ready for full-strength Sonny in every respect. Things had finally settled, and he wanted the last piece of the puzzle in place so he could finally enjoy his boyfriend.

The curtain moved, and there he was, in jeans and a tucked-in blue-and-red flannel with the sleeves rolled up to his elbows. Abe couldn't see out of the new eye, but he hoped Sonny could see him as whole again.

"Hey," Abe said with a sheepish smile.

Sonny came to him. "Hey," he said, handing him his T-shirt. They'd let him keep his jeans, and he'd already put his shoes back on.

The nurse approached. "Mr. Ellis, you did well, and it looks like the eye is settled. How does it feel?"

"Good. A little strange, not being able to see out of it. But I don't know, it feels like an eye," he finished with a shrug.

Sonny snickered, shaking his head.

"Is he always like this?"

"Always," Sonny confirmed.

Abe narrowed his eyes at Sonny playfully.

"We'll get the paperwork done, and then he's free to go," she said. "We'll give you all the pamphlets and everything so you both know what to expect as he adjusts."

Once she left the room, Sonny turned back to him.

"So, how do I look?"

Sonny came close, so close that Abe had to part his legs so Sonny could stand between them. He cupped Abe's face, turning it up to the light, smoothing his hair back. He looked back and forth between the real eye and the prosthetic, studying them. Abe waited, heart pounding, before Sonny broke into a smile. "It looks perfect," he said finally. "They match, and yet they don't. So it's perfect, natural."

Abe touched his waist then, wanting nothing more

than for this man to take him home and to finally be able to begin his life, his partnership, with him.

"You're so damn beautiful, you know that?"

Abe smiled. "All right, now you're just flattering me," he said, squeezing Sonny's sides.

Sonny chuckled, squirming.

"Oh my God, are you ticklish?" He squeezed again, and Sonny wiggled more.

"Yes. Now quit it," he said, reaching down to still Abe's hands.

Abe stopped, reaching for his shirt. "I swear, I'm dating Andy-fucking-Griffith."

"Does that make you Barney Fife?"

Abe laughed aloud at that. "Aren't you a little young for that?"

Sonny stood back, letting Abe remove the hospital gown and put his shirt on, clearly trying not to stare as he did. "You keep saying that, and yet here I am."

"I feel like I'm simultaneously dating an older and a younger man," Abe remarked, standing up.

"You're not that much older."

"I'm thirty-one," he said.

"And I'm twenty-six. That's not much."

Abe tugged at Sonny's shirt. "And yet he tucks in his shirts and goes to church with the rest of the old folks."

"You don't tuck in your shirts?" Sonny quipped.

"You callin' me old?"

Sonny planted a kiss on his lips. "Not even a little bit, Barn."

Abe snorted, pushing away from him.

* * *

Abe climbed into Sonny's truck. As he buckled his seat belt, he caught Sonny stealing another glance at him. He tossed his hair to the side and smiled at him knowingly.

"Like what you see, Sonny?"

"For the record, I always have. It's just good to see you healed."

Abe shook his head as he looked away. "Home, James," he joked.

"Yes, sir," Sonny played along, turning the radio on as they pulled away from the hospital.

They rode for a few moments in silence before Abe reached over and placed his hand on Sonny's knee. Sonny looked over at him briefly, dropping one hand from the steering wheel to hold it.

Abe squeezed his hand gently, and Sonny brought it to his lips, kissing the back of his hand. Abe felt the gesture in his chest. *This is what it feels like to be loved.* He'd had the thought several times since getting closer to Sonny. He'd thought it when Sonny showed up at the hospital right out of County, his hair still wet from the undoubtedly quick shower he'd taken before heading straight there. He'd thought it when Sonny brought him into his home and took care of him while he healed. He'd thought it when the fragmented memories began to surface from that night, when he'd been so thankful to see Sonny, knowing what helping had cost him. Over and over during the past few weeks he'd thought: *This is love. This is what it feels like to be loved and to be in love.*

"You okay?" Sonny asked, bringing him out of his thoughts.

"I'm in love," Abe said. He watched the smile, the flush on Sonny's throat and cheeks, even as he kept his eyes on the road.

"Me too."

"Anyone I know?"

"Yeah. This snappy little blond thing," Sonny said.

"Snappy?" Abe asked.

"Yeah, you know, funny, quick-witted, sarcastic."

"Aw, you nailed my best qualities." Abe waited, seeing Sonny's mouth twist. "Come on, I set you up for it. Make the joke."

"I'm gonna nail something later," Sonny said.

"I hope the fuck you do."

* * *

Sonny pulled his truck into the spot next to Abe's car in the driveway. They climbed out of the vehicle and couldn't get in the house fast enough. Sonny barely had the door unlocked and the alarm code entered before Abe was on him, pushing him inside and closing the door behind them.

"Kiss me," Abe said.

Sonny wrapped his arms around him, obliging happily. He turned, pinning Abe to the wall beside the front door, kissing him, nipping at his lips, teasing his tongue into Abe's mouth. He slid a thigh between Abe's legs, and Abe groaned into his mouth, pressing his hips forward. "You're sure you're up to—"

"I have waited weeks. *Weeks*," Abe said.

Sonny leaned his forehead against Abe's. "I know. But you just had that procedure."

"They didn't even knock me out. I'm fine, Sonny. Please."

Sonny reached down and pressed a firm hand against the front of Abe's jeans, feeling how hard he was already. Abe moaned, pushing into his hand, and Sonny kissed him again, this time with more fervor, robbing him of his breath as he rubbed him through his jeans.

"What do you want, Abe?" he asked between kisses.

"I want you to fuck me," he panted. "I want you to use everything you've got and pound me into your mattress."

Sonny smiled, undoing Abe's jeans and sliding his hand inside them to touch him, skin to skin. "Are you sure? You could have anything you wanted," Sonny said, dipping his tongue into Abe's ear.

"I want everything," Abe said, gripping Sonny's shoulders, arching into him. "I want my boyfriend to take me upstairs and just" —he paused, catching his breath —"have me."

Sonny beamed at that. He moved to sweep Abe up into his arms and do just as Abe wished, when he felt the cold press of metal against his neck.

"Don't move."

* * *

Abe froze, watching the color drain from Sonny's face.

"Get away from him. Get your hands off him," the voice behind Sonny said, and Sonny did as he was told, turning slowly.

"M-Mason—" But Mason struck Sonny across the cheek with the side of the gun in his hand, throwing him temporarily off-balance.

"Shut up," Mason sneered.

Abe stayed frozen for far longer than his instincts should've allowed. The only way he could justify it was that he truly thought Mason might shoot Sonny, and maybe, if he held perfectly still, he could delay it.

"Mason," Abe said.

"I said shut the fuck up," Mason growled, taking him in. "They fixed your face. What a shame. People could finally see how twisted and deformed you are just by looking at you."

Abe chanced a look at Sonny, who looked as confused and as sick as Abe had ever seen him.

"Aw, what's wrong, Mr. Lakes? Not so charming when people aren't charmed?"

"It was you. It's been you the whole time, hasn't it?"

"The Lord's work," Mason said. "Not that I'd expect *you* to understand. You show up on Sundays and pretend to be part of something you know isn't yours."

"Mason, put the gun down," Abe said, causing him to swing the gun back on him.

"Why? One less faggot in the world. Maybe two."

Abe heard the words, but they didn't register. Because what he was seeing was the gun. *His* gun, the revolver he carried on duty, despite all the teasing he'd endured for it. Nate was right: he did think the revolver was cool and sexy, and that's why he loved it. He was as quick with it as any standard semiautomatic handgun, but only because he'd practiced and practiced.

"I have to say, when Officer Landis started blaming Mr. Lakes for everything, I really did get a kick out of that," Mason said. "Not because I liked someone taking credit for what I was doing, but because it was like divine justice. Because really, you fags bring it all on yourselves."

Abe studied the gun, trying to remember if it had been loaded. Sonny had brought it in from the car in its case the night his truck had been vandalized, but with everything going on, Abe was almost certain the speed loader with the ammunition was still locked in the glove box of his car.

Almost certain, but not completely.

He took a deep breath and vowed to make everything right if he was correct.

"Sonny, I'm sorry."

Abe lunged at Mason, and Mason pulled the trigger.

* * *

Sonny watched it happen, certain he'd heard a blast. His legs gave out as he covered his face and closed his eyes. *Not happening, not happening, not happening*, he thought on a loop.

"Sonny? Sonny!"

Sonny opened his eyes to find Mason pinned on his front underneath Abe's knee as Abe held Mason's hands behind his back to subdue him. There was no blood, no smell of gunfire, nothing.

"I need you to call the police," Abe said.

Sonny blinked, looking around, and saw that Abe already had the gun tucked into the back of his jeans. He finally snapped out of it, reaching into his pocket for his smartphone.

"Nine-one-one, what is your emergency?"

"Uh, S-Sonny Lakes, 195 Th-Third Street, Sweetshade. I h-have a violent intruder in my home. He pulled a gun on us and —"

"Is anyone hurt?"

He looked at Abe again, then down at himself. "N-no, ma'am, no one's hurt," he said, feeling the truth of it threatening to choke him.

"All right, we're sending help. I'd like you to stay on the line with me, sir."

He nodded, realizing too late that she couldn't see him. "Yes, sorry. I'm here. I-I'll stay on the line, yes."

* * *

After the cops came and arrested Mason, after they took his and Sonny's statements, everyone left. Once Abe walked Nate and Gonzalez out, he came back in to find Sonny sitting hunched over on the couch. It was so quiet, startlingly so.

"Sonny." He stood a few feet away in case Sonny lashed out. Not that Sonny would hit him or anything like that. But he knew if he tried to touch or comfort him before he wanted it, Sonny would jerk away from him. And he couldn't bear that, not after what they'd just been through.

"You're so fucking stupid," Sonny said, his voice shaking.

"Maybe I am," Abe said. "But I was right."

"What if you weren't?" Not quite angry. Pleading, almost. "Wh-what if you were wrong and it had been loaded and he blew you away right then and there?"

Abe sat down next to him, hearing the rising panic, the bubbling up of suppressed emotion.

"He didn't."

"But if he did, Abe? What if he did, after everything?"

Abe could see him shaking, could hear the tears he was desperate to hold in, trying to be angry instead of frightened. *Because that's what he is. Angry. Because you just scared him to death.* Abe scooted closer.

195

"Sonny, I'm fine. Look at me, look."

But Sonny wouldn't. "How could you do that to me?" he asked in such a quiet, pained voice that it pierced Abe straight through the heart.

That's when he threw all holding back to the wind and crawled into Sonny's lap, straddling him so he had no choice but to face him. Sonny looked up at him, clearly caught between anger and deep hurt. "Because I love you. I took a chance, hoping you'd forgive me either way."

"I swear I heard it. I heard the gun go off…"

"You didn't," Abe said. "I know how dumb that was. I know. But I never keep the gun loaded off duty. The bullets are still locked in my glove box."

Sonny shook his head, looking away. "Still."

"Forgive me," Abe said. "Let me be your hero, Sonny. Just this once."

Sonny locked gazes with him. "It's not the same—"

"It is the same. You had no idea if I was alone on your porch, and you never hesitated."

Sonny said nothing.

"You sat in County for three days and never complained once. You've taken care of me and never complained once. Please, for the love of God, let me be the one who came to your rescue this time," he pleaded.

Sonny looked away then. That damn wall. For the first time since the beating, Abe felt Sonny slam the wall down in his face. He leaned forward, pressed his lips to Sonny's forehead, his temple.

"Please forgive me," Abe whispered. When Sonny still didn't answer, he felt his heart drop. He pulled back, trying to look into his eyes, trying desperately to get through to him. "Tell me what I have to do."

"That wasn't heroic. That was dangerous and

stupid."

"Sonny, please." He hated this, hated the desperation in his voice. "Please don't shut me out."

"You scared the hell out of me less than two hours ago," Sonny said. He sat forward, lifting him out of his lap. Sonny touched his own cheek where Mason had struck him with the gun. The small wound had scabbed over but still needed to be cleaned.

"Are you going to forgive me?"

"I need time. I need to calm down," Sonny said with an edge. "My hands are still shaking, for fuck's sake."

Abe felt it then, even if Sonny hadn't physically jerked away this time. He heard it in Sonny's voice, in his choice of words.

"I need to clean this," Sonny said, standing up. And just like that, as warm as he could be, Abe felt how cold it could become when Sonny shut him out.

Abe ran his hands through his hair, knowing he'd fucked up, completely and irrevocably. He stood as calmly and quietly as he could, then grabbed his keys and left.

Sixteen

Sonny went through the motions of his life in Sweetshade, working at Tom's, going to therapy, taking care of his house and yard. But inside, he felt the hole Abe had left. It had been nearly two weeks since everything had come to a head with Mason, and they still hadn't spoken. Everyone around him said the same things, over and over.

First, Jean.

"I know it was bad and what Abe did was really, really stupid."

"You're absolutely right," Sonny responded firmly.

"People make mistakes."

"That mistake could've gotten both of us killed."

"He's miserable, Sonny. And so are you."

Sonny met her eyes then. "Oh yeah?"

"Yeah, you are, and I hate seeing it."

"Don't you think I hate feeling this way?"

"Then forgive him."

Then, Dr. Carmichael.

"That must've been terrifying," she said after he explained it all to her.

"It was."

"Have you talked to him?"

He shook his head.

"Why not?"

"Because I…" He tried to find the words.

"Whatever you're feeling, just say it."

"Angry," he admitted.

"That's an understandable and normal thing to feel, given what you both went through."

He lifted his gaze to hers. "But?"

"There's only a 'but' if you want it to be. Do you think there is?"

"I really like him. I love him. I miss him."

"Then forgive him."

"I don't know how."

"I can understand that. It was your job to both protect people and make good decisions under stress, being a soldier and a medic. And what he did was reckless, and I can understand how that would be hard for you to reconcile."

"Very."

She waited long enough for him to look up at her again.

"But you love him. You have to decide if you love him enough to try to forgive him."

He swallowed hard, looking down at his hands. "What if I can't?"

"How about we cross that bridge when we come to it? Would you like to try to forgive him?"

He closed his eyes. "More than anything."

"Then try. We'll deal with *can't* if it happens."

* * *

Abe was just about to microwave a frozen meal when he heard a knock at the door. He frowned, walking over and peering through the peephole.

And there he was, in jeans and a T-shirt, as handsome

and sweet-faced as ever.

"Abe? It's me."

Abe steeled himself before unlocking and opening the door.

"Hey," Sonny said, hands in his pockets.

"Hey," Abe replied, hating the way he wanted to launch himself into Sonny's arms and kiss him. He missed his kisses. He missed everything.

"Can I come in?"

Abe swallowed, nodding. "Sure." He stepped aside and let Sonny in, realizing how much less tidy a person he was when he was down in the dumps. "Sorry, I wasn't expecting company." He shoved the frozen dinner back into his freezer as Sonny leaned against the kitchen bar.

"It's fine."

"So, what's up?" Abe asked, sitting on one of the barstools on the other side of the kitchen bar. *Safer to keep something between us.*

"Look at me."

Abe made himself meet Sonny's eyes then, even though it hurt. It hurt to look at him. "Wh-what..." he stammered, faltered, shaking his head. "What do you need?" He said it to the bar instead of trying to look at him again, tracing the edge of the countertop with his thumb.

"I just wanted to see you," Sonny said. "I haven't seen you in two weeks."

"I've been busy," Abe said.

Sonny nodded at that. "I wanted to ask if you'd like to come to Maryland with me for Thanksgiving. I want you to meet my family."

Abe frowned, still refusing to meet his eyes. "Why?"

"Abe..."

"Just break up with me, all right? Just do it. You came in person, which is honorable. Because God forbid Sonny Lakes do anything dishonorable."

"Abe," Sonny said again, coming around the bar to him. "I don't want to break up."

Abe looked up at him then, indignant. "You could have fooled me."

"I still love you."

"And I still love you," Abe said. "But I'm not going to keep begging you to forgive me if you won't."

Sonny came closer, and Abe wanted to recoil and fall into his arms at the same time, in near equal measures.

"I want to forgive you. I want to try and work toward it."

Abe swallowed again. "I don't think I could stand it if you tried and couldn't."

Sonny reached out then, brushed his hair back. "Trying is all I can do."

"It's not enough," Abe said, his throat and eyes stinging.

Sonny's hand fell away. "So you'd ask me to have faith in your instincts, but you won't put any faith in my ability to forgive?"

Abe felt pinned by that. He stared up into blue eyes, lighter and grayer than his own, and broke into a half-hearted smile. "Touché. But still, it's my heart on the line."

"And it was my life on the line, along with yours," Sonny countered.

"Are you going to hold that over my head every time you're upset with me?"

That seemed to knock Sonny back a few paces because he faltered. "You have to give me a chance to work at it. I can try, but I can't do it if you aren't there."

"You really think you can?"

Sonny stepped even closer, close enough to touch. To kiss. "I do. I'm already close. I just need your help."

Abe blinked away lingering tears, and Sonny cupped his face in his big, warm hands.

"Please trust me."

Abe couldn't help it. He pressed his hands over Sonny's. "Think you could learn to trust me again?"

"I do," Sonny said, stroking his thumb over Abe's cheek. "I really do."

"What can I do to help?"

"Well, first, I'd like to kiss you," Sonny said.

Abe peered up at him, his gaze darting between Sonny's eyes and his mouth. He nodded, and Sonny leaned in, touched his lips to Abe's. Just a touch at first, gentler and more tentative than their first kiss. But Abe practically melted. "Mmm, I missed kissing you," Abe murmured.

"I missed kissing you too. I've missed all of you." He nudged his hips between Abe's legs.

Abe wrapped his arms around Sonny's waist, feeling him through the soft cotton shirt, warm with his body heat. "I missed you too." He bit his lip. "What else can I do to help?"

"Well, you could let me take you on a date."

Abe looked up at him, seeing the happy eagerness in his face. "Now?"

"Unless you're too busy with that frozen-dinner thing."

"Ha-ha. We don't all have your grace in the kitchen."

Sonny smiled. "But seriously, if you have other stuff to do tonight…"

"I don't," Abe said. "What did you have in mind?"

"Well," Sonny said, "I was thinking pizza, maybe a couple of beers?"

Abe frowned playfully. "Vegan pizza?"

"It does exist," he said. "I found a place in Corpus Christi we could try together."

Abe nodded. "Okay, yeah. Should I change?"

Sonny gave him a look. "It's pizza and beer, Abe. You look fine."

"Just fine?"

Sonny chuckled at the obvious reach for a compliment, and Abe squeezed his sides. "Hey, cut it out." Sonny squirmed.

"Just fine?"

"You look amazing and you know it," Sonny said, grabbing Abe's hands so he couldn't tickle him anymore.

"You're the cutest, I swear," Abe said.

"Come on, let's go," Sonny said, holding Abe's hands as he stood.

Abe grabbed his wallet, smartphone, and keys, and followed Sonny out of the apartment.

Nestled in the cab of Sonny's truck, lulled by the classic rock coming from the radio, Abe couldn't help but be thankful as he looked over at him. He'd been convinced that Sonny would never speak to him again, and it'd hurt like hell. Not that he had the best track record with men, but Sonny was by far the best man he'd ever dated, and losing him, well…it damn near broke his heart.

Sonny looked over, seeming to sense Abe looking at him. "What?"

"Nothing, sorry." Abe looked away, feeling the flush creep into his cheeks. "Just zoned out."

Sonny reached over, offering his hand. Abe took it, grateful as Sonny squeezed it, his eyes returning to the road.

Abe wanted to lift it to his lips, wanted to kiss it like Sonny had on the way home from his procedure. But he thought better of it, knowing they couldn't just pretend nothing had happened.

They rode the rest of the way in silence, holding hands.

* * *

Sonny ordered for them after discussing their options for toppings. Abe let him choose for the most part. Sonny could tell something was cycling in Abe's mind because he'd clammed up in the truck. He brought the plates, napkins, forks, and knives over to the table Abe had chosen, and sat down. Abe had brought their beers over, but it looked like he hadn't drunk any of his yet.

"So, how's work been?" Sonny asked.

Abe scratched the back of his neck. "Well, I'm not exactly a cop anymore," he said, startling Sonny. "It's not a big deal. You can't be a cop with one eye. They're keeping me on as a dispatcher." He took a drink of his beer, attempting casualness.

"I'm so sorry."

"It's fine. How about you? How's Tom's?"

"It's good. Same old, same old."

"Jean giving you hell?"

Sonny chuckled. "Usually."

"They're a pair, she and Nate."

"Oh, I gathered that," Sonny said, taking a drink of his beer. The conversation died again, and Sonny watched the shadows on Abe's face, dimming his mood once more, felt Abe's tension as if it were a thing Abe could touch him with. *Maybe I was too pushy. Maybe he doesn't want this anymore.*

"If I've come on too strong, if you don't want this, we don't have to—"

"What?" Abe focused on him then, his gaze filled with poorly concealed fear.

"You just don't seem like yourself."

"I nearly lost my boyfriend and my job in the same couple of weeks," Abe said. "How would you seem?"

Sonny watched him look away, take another drink, his jaw clenched tight. "Like absolute hell," Sonny said. "Maybe we should get the pizza to-go?"

Abe shrugged. "Sure."

* * *

They rode back to Sonny's house in silence. Sonny carried the pizza into his kitchen and placed it in the oven, box and all.

"What're you doing?" Abe asked.

"Keeping it warm," Sonny said, rising back to his full height. "Now. Out with it."

"Out with it?"

"You're angry."

Abe stared at him. "And I'm supposed to what? Spill my guts on command because suddenly you're ready to listen?"

"Do you even want me back?"

"Are you kidding me? That's all I've wanted! I waited for you to call, to text, anything! I begged you to forgive me that night, and you wouldn't even look at me!"

"I was still in shock. Everything happened so fast, and I couldn't think—"

"You think I wasn't? I knew the risk I was taking—"

"And you took it with both our lives! I didn't have any say in that."

"I said I was sorry. Repeatedly. It was a stupid thing to do. I know that. I get it. You've made yourself abundantly clear."

"It still hurt. It still scared the hell out of me."

"Don't start with me. I believed you nearly the whole time everything was still happening with Mason, and I had no proof you weren't doing it other than my instincts. The same ones that told me the gun was empty."

Sonny nodded. "That's fair. I don't like it, and it still scares the shit out of me, but you're right. You did believe me, and you have no idea what that meant to me."

Abe studied him. "You can trust me for that but not for the other?"

"Abe, I'm trying. I'm trying to forgive it. Ask anyone who's had to put up with me for the past couple of weeks."

Abe came to him then, looking up at him. "I want you back, more than anything. But you have to forgive me."

"You would barely look at me just now."

Abe touched him, hands on Sonny's upper arms. "Because I know we can't just go back to the way things were all at once. And I wanted to. I wanted to touch and kiss and laugh like nothing ever happened. But it did, Sonny."

Sonny looked down at him.

"We have to respect that it did, or we aren't going to be able to heal."

Sonny sighed, hands on Abe's elbows, resting his forehead against Abe's. "For the record, this is when I definitely feel like the younger man. You just made more sense than I've been able to in the past two weeks."

"Stick with me," Abe said, feeling their progress opening up the lines of communication, unlocking the affection between them.

"I plan to," Sonny said.

"All right. Where's this exotic vegan pizza?"

Sonny chuckled, turning to take it back out of the oven. "We might have to zap it in the microwave a little." He placed the box on the kitchen table, opening it and setting out a couple of paper plates and napkins.

"Nah, I love cold pizza," Abe said.

Sonny wrinkled his nose teasingly.

"Ever tried it?"

"Yes, and it's awful," Sonny said, taking a few pieces onto his plate and popping them in the microwave.

"Suit yourself," Abe said, taking a bite. He chewed for a moment, savoring as Sonny watched. "So that's fake cheese, huh?"

The microwave beeped, and Sonny took his plate out, then sat down across from Abe. "Yep."

"It's not bad. There's too many veggies on this thing, though," he said, ribbing Sonny.

"Sorry." Sonny smiled sheepishly.

"It serves me right. I wasn't exactly being helpful." He took another bite.

They ate most of the pizza, their conversation circling closer and closer to normal. By the time Sonny put the leftovers in his refrigerator, they'd both relaxed significantly.

"Would you like me to take you home?" Sonny

asked.

Abe looked up at him. "I really wouldn't."

Sonny reached for his hand, and Abe stood with him.

"But maybe you should," Abe said ruefully. "Before I start throwing out mixed signals again."

Sonny looked down at him with sparkling blue eyes. "I'll do that, if that's what you want."

"What I want?"

Sonny nuzzled his hair. "Yeah. What you want," he murmured, leaning down to kiss Abe's cheek, his jaw, the place behind his ear.

Abe bit his lip, unable to stop himself from leaning into Sonny's kisses, his eyes fluttering closed.

"Tell me to stop and I will. Tell me you'd rather wait, and I will back off."

"I want you." Their eyes met, and suddenly Abe felt the heat between them, the raw ache. "I got cheated that night. I want you."

Sonny smiled before seizing his lips in another tender kiss. "Then let me take you upstairs and, how did you put it? Have you?"

Abe smiled at that, nodding eagerly. "Have me."

Seventeen

Sonny locked up and set the security alarm before following Abe upstairs.

Abe could feel Sonny's broad, looming presence behind him before he ever touched him. Abe turned when they came into Sonny's bedroom, and Sonny smiled down at him as he pulled him into his arms for a deep kiss that took Abe's breath away. Though it left him light-headed, Abe didn't dare break it. If Sonny was kissing him again, he wasn't stopping it for anything.

"Missed you," Sonny murmured between kisses. "So much."

Abe held him, smoothing his hands up Sonny's back, then down along his waist, feeling him through his T-shirt. "I missed you too. You have no idea." Abe slid his hands beneath Sonny's T-shirt, fingertips grazing his waist.

Sonny squirmed, his belly tensing. "Not funny," he said, even though his voice was warm with happiness and the likelihood of laughter.

"Sorry," Abe said. "No tickling. I'm just feeling you." He rested his forehead against Sonny's shoulder as he splayed his hands against Sonny's warm, bare skin. "You turn me on so much."

Sonny kissed Abe's temple, took one of Abe's hands, and pressed it over the front of his jeans. "You turn *me* on so much," he whispered in his ear, his breath coursing over Abe's neck, making him shiver.

Abe took the gesture as guidance and went to his knees, undoing Sonny's belt.

Sonny seemed about to relax and let him, but he must've noticed how Abe's hands shook. "Hey," he said, placing his hands over Abe's, stilling them.

Abe's hands fell away then, but he didn't get up. He just sat there on his knees, feeling desperate and stupid.

"Hey, come here, stand back up," Sonny said, reaching for him.

Abe stood, unable to meet his eyes. "I just thought that's what you wanted."

Sonny cupped Abe's face in his hands. "Look at me." When Abe met his eyes, he felt even more desperate. "I want you."

"I just don't want to mess up again. I want to make you ha-happy so you don't..." He trailed off, tears welling in his eyes for the second time that night. He swallowed against them, frustrated with himself. "So you don't leave me again."

Sonny sucked in a breath.

Abe's face burned with shame. "God. How pathetic I sound..."

"You don't sound pathetic. You sound hurt," Sonny said. "I can understand that."

"I don't know how to fix it," Abe admitted. "I just want to fix us. I want my boyfriend back."

"I haven't gone anywhere."

"Yes, you did. I understand why, but you still did," Abe said.

Sonny sat on the edge of the bed, clearly at a loss himself. "I feel like we're going in circles."

Abe chewed his lip, hoping it wasn't defeat he heard

in Sonny's voice. He could feel Sonny's eyes on him. Abe wrapped his arms around himself. "Maybe you should take me home."

Sonny reached up, touched Abe's forearm. "We don't have to have sex," Sonny said. "I just want to be close. I missed you, and I do think we can work this out, but not in a night. If you want me to take you home, I absolutely will. But I…" He shook his head. "I just want to hold you for a little while. We don't have to talk. Clearly, I'm not doing so hot with that right now."

"Me neither," Abe said.

"But I'd rather not talk in the same room," Sonny said. "I'd rather do it holding you, if you'll let me."

And just like that, Sonny articulated it when Abe had been at a loss for what he wanted for the past two weeks. Maybe talking wasn't working right then, but he dreaded suffering in silence by himself again. Tears spilled down his cheeks, and all he could do was nod as his face scrunched up. "Please," he managed.

Sonny reached for him, pulling him onto the bed with him. They lay as they always did when they slept together, Sonny on the left and Abe on the right, only this time with Abe curled up against Sonny's chest, leaving a third of the bed empty. Abe pressed himself close, burying his face against Sonny's chest, and Sonny held him tight, one arm around his back, the other cradling his head against him.

Abe thought he had a grip, tenuous though it was, until Sonny began kissing his hair, kneading and rubbing him to comfort him. Sobs of pain and relief came loose then.

"It's okay, Abe. It's okay. I'm right here, and I'm so sorry for hurting you."

Sobs wracked him, quiet but shaking him.

"I'm so sorry," Sonny whispered, over and over, along with *I love you* and *we're going to be okay.*

* * *

Sonny waited a long time as Abe let it out, feeling sympathetic pain within himself. He hadn't realized how much he'd hurt Abe. Not until then.

Several slow minutes went by, and Abe seemed to calm down. Finally, he pulled back, lifting his head.

Sonny took him in, cheeks and nose puffy, his eye bloodshot, his lips a raw flush.

"Don't look at me," Abe grumbled.

"Why not?"

"I know what I look like when I cry."

"You look like someone who's been really hurt," Sonny said, nearly choking on guilt.

"Well," Abe said with a shrug.

"I have an idea, if you want to try it," Sonny said, testing the waters.

"What is it?"

"Once a week I see a therapist for my PTSD," Sonny began. "Maybe she'd be willing to talk to us a few times together."

Abe seemed to turn it over in his mind. "Like couples' therapy?"

"Just to get us over this bump," Sonny said. "And we don't have to if you don't want to."

"It might help," Abe said. "I've never been to therapy before."

Sonny brushed Abe's hair back, watching his eyes flutter at the touch. "It's not so bad. I'm not sure if she does the couples thing, but I could email her in the morning to see if she'd be willing to help us."

"I just don't want to lose you, Sonny," Abe said, biting his lip. "I'll try anything."

Sonny scooted closer, pressing his forehead to Abe's. "Me too."

"Is she nice?"

Sonny smiled at that. "Very. I really liked my therapist in Maryland, and they're colleagues."

"How have your nightmares been?"

"Better. I haven't really had any in a few weeks. I had some stress dreams when we weren't talking, but nothing like... Well, I'm sure you remember."

"So, even if we don't have sex," Abe began, "can I just sleep here with you?"

Sonny kissed his temple. "Of course you can."

Abe rose up and kissed his lips once. "Thank you."

They took turns showering.

"Here," Sonny said, handing Abe a spare toothbrush.

Abe chuckled.

"What?"

"Nothing. Just you," Abe said. "Always organized and prepared."

After getting cleaned up, they resettled in Sonny's bed. Only this time, they were in shorts and T-shirts, under the covers, their body heat mingling to create a cozy, shared warmth.

Abe nestled back against Sonny's chest, and Sonny wrapped an arm around his waist, pulling Abe into the natural cradle of his body.

"I love you, you know?" Sonny kissed Abe's shoulder once through his shirt.

Abe folded an arm over Sonny's, lacing their fingers

together. "I love you too."

* * *

The next morning, Abe woke first. His neck and shoulders were stiff from lying in the same position for so long, but he could hear Sonny's steady breath as he continued to sleep, curled against him from behind.

Abe wiggled as gently as he could to relieve the ache in his neck and shoulders, and accidentally brushed Sonny's cock — his very erect, very warm cock. He smiled, blushing, shaking his head. Sure, he woke up with the proverbial morning wood too, but…damn. Abe pushed his ass back into Sonny's lap, nudging him again.

"Mmm," Sonny groaned in his sleep, flexing the arm wrapped around Abe's middle.

Abe chuckled, feeling Sonny absently press himself closer. He felt none of the desperation of the night before and all the desire as he rubbed backward.

"Mmm, what're you doing?" Sonny asked, his voice thick with sleep.

"Observing how excitable you are in the morning," Abe said with a snicker.

"You're nothing but trouble. And so early." Sonny nuzzled Abe's nape, sliding a hand into Abe's shorts.

"And here I thought the military man would be up with the sun," he remarked, sighing as Sonny's hand wrapped around his member.

"Was I not?" he joked, rubbing his palm against the underside of Abe's cock.

"My word, Sonny Lakes, was that a dirty joke?"

"Only the dirtiest for you, dear."

"I'm going to hold you to that," Abe tossed back,

even as Sonny began pressing wet, sucking kisses to his neck, his hand in his shorts, working him with surprising finesse for a man just woken up. He reached behind him into Sonny's shorts and found the thick, rigid member that had pressed against his ass.

Sonny groaned again, a deep rumble in his chest that only turned Abe on more, and nipped Abe's neck. "Do you want to make love?"

Anyone else and it would've sounded awkward and stilted. But when Sonny asked it in those words, Abe melted. Such a big, broad man, so well endowed and powerfully built, and he used words like *make love*. "Please."

They both sat up at nearly the same moment, helping each other out of their sleep clothes before returning to the bed.

Sonny guided Abe over onto his front. "Okay?" he asked.

Abe nodded, relaxing on his stomach.

He felt Sonny's gaze on him as he lay against the mattress, hands resting on the bed and pillows beneath his shoulders. Sonny's weight shifted on the bed as he presumably reached for the lube, and at the sound of the cap popping open, Abe lifted his ass into the air slightly.

"Does that thing have a mind of its own?" Sonny asked, smoothing a hand over the curves of Abe's ass, squeezing each cheek in passing.

"I just...fuck. I'm too horny and too under-caffeinated to come up with a good comeback."

Sonny laughed at that. "I promise we'll take care of both." He crawled between Abe's legs, nudging them apart. "Ass up."

Abe lifted his bottom again and felt Sonny's touch

almost immediately. Fingers slicked with lubricant slid over his hole, around and around at first, then gently testing, teasing with soft presses against his rim, not quite penetrating him.

"Does that feel good?"

"Uh-huh," Abe murmured, pushing back against the delicious threat of intrusion.

"Relax," Sonny said. "I'm going to give you everything you want."

Abe felt the flush spread from his chest to his throat and face and wondered if Sonny could see it. He started to look over his shoulder as Sonny pressed the first digit inside him. "Ooh," Abe moaned, pushing against it, wanting. Sonny twisted his finger inside Abe, lubricating him and coaxing him open in the same motions.

"Your ass is so perfect," he said, carefully adding another finger. "So tight and yet so willing to relax for me."

"You never give me reason to be any other way," Abe said. "You take care of me better than anyone ever h-has like this."

Sonny added one last finger, and Abe gave in to the final, tingling stretch.

"Sonny, please," he groaned softly, stars dancing against his eyelids as Sonny's fingers grazed his prostate purely by chance. Not a focused effort, just enough to make his breath hitch.

And just like that, the fingers were gone. He heard Sonny open and close the bedside table drawer once more, heard the crinkle of the condom wrapper. *Always the sweet, cautious gentleman.*

Sonny leaned down over Abe, and he felt Sonny's thick, broad tip press against his hole. "Ready for me?"

216

Abe nodded, wanting him so badly, he ached.

Sonny entered him in one long, smooth move that tried Abe's limits without breaking them. Abe writhed as Sonny began to fuck him with slow, deliberate strokes.

Abe buried his face against the pillows, so thankful for the sensation of not only being filled, but being filled by this man, that he nearly cried out from that alone. A good lover and, though flawed and damaged, a wonderful man.

"You should see yourself, Abel," Sonny said. "You're flushed down your back and, God, the way you move with me…" Sonny lowered himself to Abe's back, clearly needing to be close too.

"S-Sonny," Abe moaned at the change of position, at how wholly more intimate it felt. He reached behind him, cupping Sonny's ass in his hands, feeling the muscles bunch as Sonny thrust powerfully deep.

"That's right," Sonny panted in his ear. "Hands on me." He reached beneath Abe then to touch him, and found the spot of precome he'd leaked onto the sheets.

"Sorry," Abe said, embarrassed.

"Don't you dare," Sonny replied. "You're so damn sexy."

"Where on earth have you been?" Abe asked, wriggling excitedly between Sonny's hand stroking him firmly, and his cock steadily thrusting in his ass.

"I'm here now," Sonny said. "Oh, oh shit," he swore, slowing, obviously close.

"No, let it come," Abe said. "Let it." And Sonny did, gripping Abe's hips and pounding his climax into Abe's ass. Abe took it happily, grateful for feeling Sonny lose control a little.

If he'd been expecting Sonny to roll off and leave him

to finish himself, he'd been sorely mistaken. The moment his orgasm subsided, Sonny withdrew and flipped Abe onto his back.

Abe lay there, flushed and erect, gasping as Sonny descended on him.

Sonny swallowed his cock down, his fingers slipping into Abe's ass, finding his prostate at once.

"Sh-shit, Sonny!" Abe ran a hand through Sonny's dark hair, almost gripping it before he realized what he was doing. "Fuck. Sorry."

Sonny chuckled, coming up for a breath. "I don't think I can do what you do, but you can still touch me, encourage me," Sonny said, nuzzling the head of Abe's cock with his lips. "If you want." He winked as he took him again, and Abe ran his fingers through Sonny's hair, kneading and gripping lightly. Sonny tapped his gland, sucking Abe with a passion he could hear.

"Oh, oh fuck," Abe panted. "Close, I'm close!"

And just when he thought Sonny would pull off, maybe jerk him to the finish, he doubled down and held still, his throat working Abe, his fingers coaxing him along until he came in several sharp bursts. Sonny swallowed everything, milking him until Abe squirmed, oversensitive in his postorgasmic state.

"Shit," Abe panted as Sonny rose up to remove the condom, tying it off and placing it in the trash. Abe reached for him when he returned, snuggling against his chest. "I fucking love you."

Sonny laughed, holding him close. "I love you too."

* * *

After getting cleaned up and dressed, Sonny waited for

Abe downstairs.

Abe came down, looking just as handsome, if slightly ruffled, in yesterday's clothes. "What, no coffee?"

"I figured I'd buy you a nice strong coffee on the way back to your place," Sonny said, wrapping an arm around his waist, kissing him once. "Sweet Bean?"

"If it's up to me, Starbucks," Abe said.

Sonny chuckled. "Starbucks it is."

They walked out to Sonny's truck and climbed in. Sonny started it up and cringed as the radio came on. "Rich Girl" by Hall and Oates. He moved to change it, and Abe nudged him.

"Leave it," he said playfully.

Sonny smirked at him. "Really?"

"Yes, really," Abe said, beginning to sing along despite Sonny's distaste. "Come on, you know the words. Sing with me, Mr. Rock 'n' Roll."

Sonny laughed as he backed out of his driveway, heading for Starbucks. Abe serenaded him for the remainder of the song, wiggling in his seat.

"Rich Girl" gave away to Queen's "We Will Rock You," and Abe turned it up. "Now you have to sing," he teased, stomping and clapping in time with the song. "I'll do this part, you do Freddie's."

And even though just a few months ago, if you'd told him he'd be singing along with his favorite band next to his boyfriend on their way to grab coffee after some amazing sex, he'd have called you crazy, Sonny did just that.

Eighteen

After dropping Abe off at his apartment, coffee in hand, Sonny drove back home. Gone were the days of worrying that he'd return to find his house damaged or broken into, and for that he was grateful.

Once inside, he sat down with his smartphone and typed an email to Dr. Carmichael.

> *Dr. Carmichael,*
> *I hope you're well. I had a thought and was wondering if you could help me. Abe and I are having some trouble seeing eye to eye over what happened with Mason. We want to work things out, but every time we talk about it, it feels like we get caught in the same argument.*
> *Would you be willing to have a few sessions with both of us? If you are, I have no problem paying extra for it. If not, do you have any colleagues you'd recommend for couples' therapy?*
> *Either way, I appreciate your help.*
> *Thanks,*
> *Sonny Lakes*

He read it a few times to make sure he was clear and kind in his request before sending it.

Satisfied, he sat back on his couch, sipped his coffee—an iced soy latte, since he'd grown bored of the black-coffee phase—and hoped that this leveling off he was finally feeling wasn't false hope.

He was about to go upstairs and change the sheets on his bed and start the wash when his phone pinged.

Sonny,

I am well, thank you. I would love to meet Abe and help you both work through this issue. It would be a bit more expensive, but we can discuss that at our next session.

I do want to say how proud I am that you'd reach out for this and that you're both willing to work through this with therapy. It speaks volumes of how far you've come and the type of partner you have.

See you Thursday,
Dr. Carmichael

He beamed as he texted Abe to let him know: *Hey there. Dr. Carmichael says she'll do it. I have a personal session Thurs. and will nail down the details with her then. Is there a day/time that works best for you?*

Abe responded a few minutes later: *That's awesome! Fridays are my late shift, so we could do Friday AM if that works for you?*

Sonny responded eagerly: *Works for me! I'll check with her Thursday and let you know if it works for her.*

He hesitated, wanting to thank Abe, yet without calling attention to how open he was being. He didn't want to make Abe feel weird, but he was thrilled they were both willing to work at it.

Thanks, Abe. Really. It means a lot.

He cringed as he sent the text.

I love you, Abe replied.

Sonny felt that in his chest. No heart emojis, nothing else. Just three simple words that formed the most solid reassurance Sonny had ever felt.

I love you too.

With that, he clicked the phone screen off and set off upstairs to clean.

Sonny picked Abe up on Friday morning, a cup of coffee waiting for him in the cupholder.

Abe climbed into Sonny's truck. "Hey."

"Hey." Sonny leaned over to kiss him, and Abe met his lips with a sweet good-morning kiss. "For you," he said, pointing to the coffee, and Abe smiled.

"Perfect."

Sonny backed out onto the road. "You ready for this?"

Abe bit his lip. "I think so."

"Nervous?"

Abe looked over at him. "A bit."

"Me too," Sonny admitted.

"Don't tell me that," Abe said, poking him in the side.

"No tickling while I'm driving," Sonny said, laughing as he leaned away briefly.

"You're supposed to say, 'Therapy's not scary, Abe, don't worry.'"

"It's not scary. It can be daunting, though," Sonny said. "But this is different. It's both of us going together."

Abe took a drink of his coffee. "You paid attention the other day."

Sonny winked at him. "Of course I paid attention. How am I supposed to surprise you with coffee if I don't know your order?"

Abe rolled his eyes, even as he blushed. "God."

* * *

Sonny pulled into the parking lot and was able to get a spot near the door.

Abe stepped out of the truck, coffee in hand. He looked at the small building, biting his lip nervously, wiping sweat from his palm onto his jeans.

Sonny came around the truck. "Ready?"

Abe nodded, foregoing any jokes to ease his nerves. It was time to show Sonny that he took this seriously. "Let's go."

Sonny held the door for Abe, following him inside. They only waited a few moments before a woman came through the office door behind the reception desk.

"Sonny," she said. He stood, and Abe followed suit, feeling his adrenaline spike. *Maybe that coffee wasn't such a good idea.* "And you must be Abel." She held out her hand for him, and he took it, wincing at the sweat on his palm.

"Sorry," he said, pulling away from the handshake, wiping his palm on his jeans again.

"It's all right," she said warmly. "You're nervous, and that's okay."

They walked back to her office together. Sonny patted him on the back, and he looked up at him, smiling even though it felt strained.

He and Sonny sat on the small sofa across from Dr. Carmichael, who sat in an armchair.

"It's so nice to finally meet you, Abel. Put a face to a name."

"Just Abe," he said.

She smiled. "Abe, then. Would you like to tell me a little about yourself?"

He swallowed, feeling both of them looking at him. "What do you mean?"

"I'll go first," she said. "My name is Dr. Carmichael, and I've lived here in Texas my whole life. I've been practicing psychiatry for fifteen years."

"Well, uh, my name is Abe Ellis, and I've lived here my whole life too. In Sweetshade, I mean. I was a cop there for the past ten years, but because of my eye, I'm a dispatcher now."

"How long have you been seeing each other?"

He and Sonny looked at each other, and Sonny said, "About a month? Six weeks?"

"Jesus, it feels longer than that," Abe said.

"In what way?" she asked.

"I didn't mean in a bad way. But so much has happened," Abe said, stumbling over his words and how they could be construed.

"I didn't think you meant in a bad way," she said reassuringly. "Are you happy with Sonny?"

Abe nodded. "Very."

She turned to Sonny. "How about you?"

Sonny smiled. "I am."

"But obviously, you're here for a reason."

Abe's neck and shoulders tensed, and he had to remind himself to relax.

"Why are we here, Abe?"

Abe cringed. "Because I fucked up." He looked up at Dr. Carmichael, flushing red. "Sorry, messed, I messed up."

She smiled. "Swearing is okay, especially if it helps you express yourself as honestly as possible and you're not swearing at anyone."

"Okay."

"What do you think you messed up?"

"I…" He stopped, took a deep breath. "I took a

chance and put Sonny and myself in danger."

She looked to Sonny. "Is that how you feel too?"

Sonny looked over at Abe before turning back to her. He nodded.

"By taking a chance, do you mean you thought the gun Mason had wasn't loaded and you moved to disarm him?"

Abe winced. "Yes."

"Sonny, how did you react to that?"

"It scared me. I-I thought I heard the gun go off. I know I hallucinated it, probably from the stress of the situation, but it felt so real. I thought—" He drew a deep breath. "I thought Mason shot him. I thought I was next, and I wasn't in the right position or frame of mind to stop him."

"Abe, you acted on instinct?"

"Well, sort of. After I got hurt and was staying with Sonny and the harassment continued, I asked Sonny to bring my service gun in from my car." He shifted in his seat. "I should back up. When Sonny's house was broken into the first time, I offered him one of my handguns for protection, and he refused it. Which was fine. I understood. But from then on, when I was at his house, I'd leave my service gun locked in the glove box in my car, unloaded, the ammunition next to it. When I asked him to bring in the gun after another incident at his house while I was staying with him, I never checked to see if he loaded it."

"So you assumed he didn't."

"I had to assume he'd leave it unloaded, as it was in its case when he brought it in. Guns seemed to make him nervous, so, I guess, I didn't think he'd handle it more than was necessary."

"Sonny, how do you feel about that?"

Sonny looked over at Abe again, but Abe wouldn't meet his eyes. "I think a lot of assumptions were made. I mean, Mason was unstable, so I wouldn't have wanted to gamble on whether or not he'd load a gun before wielding it."

Abe wrapped his arms around himself.

"Abe, I have a feeling a lot of your job was based on listening to your gut and trusting your instincts. And a lot of times, that served you well. Is that fair?"

"Sure."

"And, Sonny, as an army medic, you adhered to procedure and protocol, even when it didn't make complete sense or you couldn't see the whole picture. Is that fair?"

"It is."

Dr. Carmichael regarded them both. "I see two very different men, from very different backgrounds and lives, trying to make sense of each other right now. And in this case, it's not only understandable, but obvious why you can't quite see eye to eye."

"I don't see how that helps, Doc," Abe remarked.

"Abe…"

"No, he's entitled to feel that way, Sonny. And it's okay, Abe. You're right. It was an observation, not a solution. Would you both agree, though, that it's clear why you're having trouble getting over this bump?"

Sonny nodded, and Abe turned to him. "If it's so obvious, then why did you shut me out?"

"Deep breaths, Abe," Dr. Carmichael said.

Abe felt at a loss, leaning forward, running his hands through his hair.

"Although, it is a good question."

Sonny looked between the two of them, and Dr. Carmichael nodded. He said, "Because it had just happened. He wanted —"

"Don't talk about him like he's not here. He's right here, Sonny. Talk *to* him."

Sonny turned to Abe. "It'd just happened, and you were begging me to forgive you, and I needed time. I was shook up and needed to process what happened."

"And, Abe, what did you want in that moment? There's no wrong answer, even if it's irrational."

"I wanted you to forgive me. I thought I'd saved you — both of us. I took a chance and I was right, and I solved a very big problem in your life. But you wouldn't even look at me, Sonny."

"All right, deep breaths, both of you. Think about what the other has said. So often, we get caught up in being right, being justified, in having the perfect response to an argument. But if you love each other and want to get through this, then you must try to see it from each other's perspectives. You don't have to agree completely, just see it. Feel it. Try to understand it."

Abe thought it through. Sonny's shock, Sonny's need for space, for time and quiet to process it. *Maybe I was too quick to dismiss him. Maybe I assumed he'd broken up with me when really, he simply needed me to be patient.*

"Any thoughts?"

Abe said, "I'm impatient, I know I am. And when I don't get what I want, I jump to conclusions. Like he'd broken up with me. Like he was mad at me and didn't want to talk to me anymore. Like he thought I was stupid."

"I don't think you're stupid."

"You said I was," Abe said, low, not meeting his eyes.

227

"Did you, Sonny?"

* * *

Sonny felt the attention shift to him. "Right after, when he kept asking me to forgive him, I think I said what he did was stupid and dangerous."

"Do you think Abe is stupid?"

Sonny looked over at Abe, wanting to touch him, to hold him. "No, I don't. I was upset, and my words came out wrong."

Abe met his gaze.

"I don't think you're stupid, Abe. You scared me, but it doesn't mean I think you're stupid. I'm sorry I ever said that."

Abe blinked against tears. He turned back to Dr. Carmichael, smiling through them. "He doesn't think I'm stupid."

"For the record, I don't either. I think your instincts are razor sharp. But I also think that Sonny's personality and experience don't exactly lend themselves well to understanding or fully accepting instinct for situations like this. Is that fair?"

Sonny nodded.

"I didn't think it through. I just did it," Abe said, and Sonny reached for him then, pulling him close.

Abe wrapped his arms around him. "I'm so sorry."

"No, I'm sorry," Sonny replied. "I didn't mean it."

Dr. Carmichael let them have a moment, and Sonny caught her smiling.

"Sorry," he said, pulling back.

"No, no, this is good. This is excellent progress."

"It seems so silly now," Abe said.

"Sometimes, you can't see it because you're too deep in it," she said. "I do have some suggestions. One, Sonny, when you need space to process, tell Abe that. Try to stay calm and reassure him you're not running away."

Sonny nodded.

"And, Abe, you have to trust him. Pushing too hard can make things worse. Try to accept Sonny's need for space. If you're feeling insecure, tell him. I'm sure he could reassure you until he's ready to talk. Right?"

"I think so," Sonny said.

"I can do that," Abe said.

She beamed. "Good. Very good. I want you both to digest this, maybe talk about it in a couple of days. If you'd like another session, let me know."

They got up, shook her hand, and she led them back out.

"It was nice to finally meet you, Abe. Take care, you two."

"We will," Abe said, following Sonny out.

They climbed back into Sonny's truck. Sonny buckled his seat belt, and Abe followed suit as Sonny started the truck. He pulled out of the parking lot, heading for Abe's apartment. Once they were out on the highway, he looked over at Abe and saw him chewing his lip, pointedly looking out the window.

Maybe it didn't work as well as I'd hoped. He pulled off onto the shoulder, safely out of the way of the late-morning traffic, and put the vehicle in park. "Abe, look at me."

Abe turned slowly, wiping his face.

"Are we okay?"

"Yes. I think so." He shook his head, catching tears

with his hand. "I looked over at you during that session a few times and..." He trailed off, swallowing thickly.

Sonny couldn't decide whether he was carefully choosing his words, or if getting them out around his emotions was tripping him up.

"And what?"

"It's just, no one's ever cared enough, you know? I know that wasn't cheap. And therapy, God, it has a stigma, you know?" He looked up at Sonny, tears welling.

Sonny unbuckled himself and scooted closer, pulling Abe into a fierce hug. "We're human and banged up in our own ways. Sometimes it's gonna be work. But I'm not afraid of work."

"Me neither, with you," Abe said, cupping Sonny's face in his hands, touching his forehead to his.

"We're gonna be okay," Sonny said, pressing his hands over Abe's. "We are okay."

"I love you, Sonny."

"I love you too," Sonny said, and kissed him. "You okay?"

Abe nodded. "Don't suppose you have any napkins in here or anything?"

Sonny popped the glove box open, and there was a small, travel-sized pack of tissues. He handed them to Abe.

"Oh, dear God, of course you'd have the real deal," Abe said, peeling the packet open and taking one. "Organized and prepared, that's my guy."

Sonny chuckled, moving back into his seat and buckling up. "Sweet and snarky, that's mine." He pulled back onto the highway. "Want a refill?"

Abe blew his nose somewhat loudly, and Sonny snorted.

"Nice."

"I think I'm adequately caffeinated. Thanks, though."

"Mind if I swing by Sweet Bean?"

Abe eyed him curiously. "Why do you like that place so much?"

"They have vegan donuts," Sonny said, blushing slightly. "I go there enough that they've started making a few things I can eat."

"This I gotta see," Abe ribbed him.

"Ha-ha. You won't be able to tell the difference," Sonny said. He felt Abe look over at him, and smiled to himself when he took his hand. *We're going to be just fine.*

Epilogue

Two Months Later...

Abe, despite his nerves, had fallen asleep during their flight and didn't wake up until Sonny nudged him awake. "Hey, we're here," he said gently.

Abe looked around, confused for a moment.

"Come on, I'll buy you a Starbucks on the way out of the airport," Sonny said.

"Speaking my language," Abe remarked around a yawn as he stood, taking his carry-on bag from Sonny.

They made their way off the airplane, and Abe peered out the windows. "Damn. No snow," he said, snapping his fingers for effect.

"It's only November. And you never know; it's in the forecast while we're here," Sonny said, walking side by side with him to baggage claim. They'd managed to share one large checked bag between them, supplementing with their own carry-on bags. "Here, you wait for the suitcase. I'll get the coffee," Sonny said, setting his bag down next to Abe's and kissing his cheek in the process.

Abe leaned into it, still thrilled when Sonny did that. "All right, I'll be here." He watched Sonny go, handsome and tall and all his. He turned back to the luggage carousel and waited for their bag to come through. Surprisingly, it didn't take long to spot the large black suitcase with a blue ribbon tied through the main zippers.

He'd teased Sonny about it, but observing all the near-identical bags, it did make it stand out. He pulled it from the carousel and set it on its rollers next to their other bags. He slung his backpack over his shoulders and was about to place Sonny's against the handle of the suitcase to go find him, just as he returned.

"That was quick," Sonny said, handing Abe his iced brew. He picked up his backpack before taking the suitcase and trailing it behind them as they walked away.

"Your ribbon idea worked," Abe said before taking his first sip.

"I promise, there's always a method to the madness."

"That much I've gathered," Abe said.

They made their way to one of the car rental desks and began the process of picking up the car Abe had booked for them. Sonny had taken care of the airfare, so Abe booked and paid for the rental car. Sonny had mentioned that one of his sisters or his mother could've picked them up — would've been happy to, in fact — but Abe had insisted. *"I don't want my first interaction with your family to be one of those awkward how-was-your-flight conversations spoken over their shoulder while they try to drive,"* Abe had said, and Sonny had surrendered without protest.

Once everything with the car was taken care of, they let the representative walk them around the car to note any damage before they left with it. The cold hit them then. By the time the rep finished and handed him the key, Abe was shivering. They loaded their bags into the SUV. "Here, you drive. You know the way better."

Sonny took the key. "Of course. Come on, before you freeze," he joked.

Abe quickly climbed inside and shut the door behind

him, and Sonny chuckled as he started the SUV.

Abe turned the heat on full blast and leaned forward, holding his hands over one of the vents. "Think he could've taken longer?"

Sonny smiled. "It's only about forty degrees."

Abe shuddered as the heat warmed his hands. "There's no way. It's gotta be at least freezing out there." He sat back in the seat and buckled up.

Sonny did the same. "You ready for this?"

Abe looked over at him and nodded. "Yeah, I think so. I'm ready to meet your family. See if I can charm them the way you charmed my folks."

About forty-five minutes later, Sonny pulled the SUV into the driveway of a two-story country house. Just as he put the vehicle in park, one of the girls—Abe assumed it was the youngest, Leigh—darted out the front door and bounded up to the driver's side.

Sonny climbed out, and she immediately hugged him. Abe watched as Sonny embraced his little sister, and it choked him up a little, making him think of Rich.

Soon. He knew Rich's time in prison was coming to an end and he'd be out. And then Abe would get to do this with him.

He climbed out of the SUV and came around to the driver's side where they stood.

"Leigh, this is—"

"Abe!" Leigh exclaimed, throwing her arms around him next. Abe hugged her back, surprised at first. "It's so great to finally meet you!"

Abe caught Sonny's gaze over her shoulder, and Sonny shrugged, clearly pleased.

"He's told me so much about you," Leigh said as she

pulled back.

"Oh, uh, same," Abe said.

"Don't worry, all good," she said.

Abe turned on the charm. "Aw, shoot, that's no fun."

Leigh laughed, turning back to Sonny. "Come on, Mom and Maddy are waiting."

As they followed Leigh up to the house, Sonny reaching for Abe's hand. Abe looked up at him, and Sonny smiled, leaning down to kiss his cheek.

"You're doing great," he said, low enough that only Abe could hear.

* * *

Sonny sat at the kitchen table, watching the three women prepare food for the following day, each one talking and asking Abe questions in turn. He watched Abe begin to relax, answering them and talking with less and less noticeable tension in his voice and body.

Leigh made them hot chocolate on the stove. "Are you allergic to soy, Abe?"

"Nope. In fact, this one's even had me try tofu."

"What did you think?" Maddy asked, eyebrow arched.

"It's not bad. Not gonna replace steak for me anytime soon, but…" He trailed off, winking at Sonny.

Sonny chuckled. "Wouldn't want it to, unless you made that decision on your own."

"Tofu creeps me out," Maddy said.

"And the alternative doesn't?"

"Shh! I know, I don't need gory details," she said, hands up.

Leigh served them each a mug of hot chocolate,

giving one first to her brother, then the other to Abe. Abe held her hand for a moment. "Wouldn't happen to have any Baileys around here, would you?"

"I knew I liked you," Leigh said with a smile. She opened one of the higher cabinets and brought down a fresh bottle of Baileys.

Abe poured a shot into his hot chocolate and tasted it. "Perfect," he said, handing her the bottle.

She offered it to Sonny, but Sonny declined it. He didn't want anything to cloud his memory of this afternoon, watching his family and boyfriend bond and get along.

"So, we have the turkey breast; sorry, Sonny. We have the vegan roast; sorry, everyone else," Maddy began teasingly.

"Ha-ha," Sonny replied.

"Vegan green-bean casserole," Leigh said with pride.

"Sweet-potato casserole with surprisingly good vegan marshmallows," Maddy continued.

Abe looked to Sonny, incredulous. "Vegan marshmallows? What the f-sorry." He looked to Jo. "Sorry, ma'am. What in the world is in marshmallows?"

"Horse's hooves," Leigh said automatically.

"Leigh!" Jo exclaimed.

"What? It's true! Right, Sonny?"

Sonny shrugged with a smile. "Not wholly inaccurate."

"My stuffing," Jo continued, coming to sit next to her son.

"And regular, homemade macaroni and cheese," Maddy said, sitting down as well. "Pumpkin pie too."

"Actually, ladies, could we have a couple of hours with the oven at some point today?"

"Why? What're we missing?" Maddy asked.

"Pecan pie," Abe said. "My mom always makes it."

"Oh, sweetie," Jo said, turning to Sonny. "Why didn't you tell us? We could've made it."

"Abe says that, as a Texan tradition, he wanted to be the one who made it," he explained. "I'll help, of course."

Abe smiled sheepishly. "I'm not the best cook, so he's my safeguard."

"So, Abe, you're from Texas?" Maddy asked over her mug of hot chocolate.

"I am. Born and raised in Sweetshade."

"And you're a police officer?" Jo asked.

Sonny cringed. "Mom."

"No, it's okay," Abe said, placing a hand over Sonny's.

"Oh dear, I forgot," she said. "He told me about the job switch. I'm sorry, Abe."

"No, ma'am, it's okay, really. I'm a dispatcher now. Which I guess, in the grand scheme of things, is all right."

"It has to be safer," Jo said, the embarrassed flush fading from her cheeks.

Sonny sat back, watching Abe answer their questions, growing more and more relaxed with his family. It made Sonny feel good, secure. He'd found himself looking over at Abe several times, admiring him, when he caught Leigh's eye just beyond Abe. She rolled her eyes, obviously knowing she'd just caught him ogling his boyfriend. He smiled, shrugging one shoulder.

* * *

Sonny and Abe went into town later that evening to get the ingredients for the pecan pie. Mary had given Abe the recipe, already veganized by her.

"It was sweet of her to do that," Sonny said.

Abe narrowed his eyes at him. "Why do I get the feeling that my mother is sweet on my boyfriend?"

Sonny nudged him. "She's just being nice."

"You know, I'd almost gotten comfortable being her favorite. And here this tall, dark, handsome thing walks in and upends everything," Abe teased him.

Sonny leaned over and placed his mouth near Abe's ear, his hand against Abe's bottom. "I'll upend something later if you don't cut it out."

Abe wiggled against his hand. "Promise?"

"You're full of sass today," Sonny said with a chuckle.

"I didn't expect your family to like me so much," Abe said. "It put me in a good mood."

Sonny kissed his cheek. "Me too."

They'd gathered the ingredients in their cart, Sonny's eyes going wide when Abe loaded the pecans into it.

"That many?"

"That's what Mom does. It's a Texas thing."

Sonny smiled. "Whatever you say, Tex."

"Don't call me that," Abe said, wrinkling his nose. Sonny winked, and Abe arched an eyebrow. "Unless you'd like me to call you sunshine."

"No, I wouldn't like that," he said with an exaggerated grimace.

"All right, then, let's get out of here before it gets anymore nuts." He nudged Sonny. "Get it?"

Sonny shook his head. "Let's get out of here before you get anymore slap-happy."

That evening, they assembled the pie. Abe really

wanted to try and make the pie on his own, so Sonny mostly read the recipe and opened the ingredients for Abe as Abe worked.

After a time, Abe placed it in the oven and huffed the stray strands off his forehead. "Well, it looked right. We can only hope now."

Just then, Jo came into the kitchen.

"You boys finishing up?"

"Yes, ma'am," Abe said.

"Sonny, why don't you let us clean up. Leigh might like some time with her brother?"

Abe met Sonny's eyes, nodding. "We've got it. Go on."

Abe cleaned up what little mess they'd made — it was amazing to him how having Sonny at his side had made the whole trying-to-cook thing a lot less daunting and messy. Jo closed the door, gathered the ingredients and leftovers, and put them away.

"Abe, I wanted to talk to you a little, just us," she began, leaning against the kitchen counter.

"I thought so," he said, sitting down at the kitchen table.

"You're a good man for not shying away from it," she said, smiling. "So, what are your intentions for my son?" She asked it with a stern face that caused Abe's stomach to flip.

"Well, uh, I…"

She broke into a laugh. "I'm just teasing you."

He put his hand over his heart in exaggerated relief. "Jeez, Mrs. Lakes, put a guy on the spot."

"Call me Jo," she said. "No, I can see that Sonny is happier than I've seen him in a very long time, and I know at least some of that is because of you."

"I hope so," Abe said. "I hope I make him happy."

"Sweetie, you didn't see him before," she said, her eyes becoming sad. "I'm not sure what he's told you, but I'm sure you know about his service and what came after."

Abe nodded. "He told me. I think he told me everything."

She swallowed, blinking a few times. "He was so lost and upset, and I just didn't know how to help him."

"It's not your fault, Jo," Abe said, touching her hand. "Sometimes we just don't know how to help."

She sniffed. "You've known someone like Sonny?"

"Not exactly, but...my older brother. He's not a veteran, but he did get lost once. Drugs and life. He's in prison currently."

"You poor thing," Jo said.

"I miss him a lot. Sonny kind of reminds me of him sometimes. Not that I think Sonny is like an inmate; that's not what I meant."

Jo chuckled. "I didn't think so."

"Just that stubbornness, you know? That difficulty asking for help. Rich is like that." He shook his head, trying to dismiss the train of thought from his mind. "Sonny's better at it now, though. Therapy, asking for help, it doesn't seem to scare him."

"Sometimes I think he scared himself so badly that it set him straight about all that," she said. "But I do know one thing for certain, and that's that you make him happy. I could see it in his face, and you can't know how happy that makes me."

"I promise you, I will do everything I can to keep him happy," he vowed.

"No, no, keep him on his toes. Make him laugh. Make

him think. Keep him happy, yes, but keep him alive and aware. Because that's what I've seen since you both got here. The color is back in his face and eyes." She shook her head, tears welling.

"I plan on all of that," he said, smiling. "Believe me, Miss Jo, he's at his best after a good laugh."

She wiped her eyes. "That he is. All right, I'm done with the motherly interrogation. I just wanted to know you a little better." She stood, and he stood with her, hugged her.

"Of course. I'm glad. Thank you for having me, by the way."

"You're quite welcome. Now go on, let's see what kind of mischief Sonny and Leigh are up to."

* * *

Sonny and Leigh were standing by the front window in the living room when Abe and Jo found them.

"He's a good one," Jo said. "Didn't crack under pressure at all."

Abe smiled at Sonny, who held out his hand. "Come here. I want to show you something."

Abe came to him, taking his hand, letting Sonny guide him to the window beside him.

"It's snowing," Sonny said. When Abe said nothing, he looked over, and the innocent awe of a grown man seeing snow for the first time took his breath away.

"Can we go out in it? Just for a minute?"

Sonny nodded. They grabbed their coats from behind the door and went out into the front yard.

Abe looked up into the darkening sky as the tiny flurries came down around them.

"Pretty, isn't it?"

"It really is." Abe held out his hand, the tiny flakes dissolving instantaneously as they made contact with his skin.

"You've never seen snow before, have you?"

Abe shook his head.

"It's just November flurries. I don't think it'll stick too much."

Abe brushed his hand off on his jeans. "Too bad. I'd love to throw a snowball or two sometime."

Sonny approached him, wrapped his arms around Abe. "Maybe we could come back during the winter, if you're really interested in seeing some snow."

"So long as it's not Christmas," Abe said. "My mom would kill me."

"No, not Christmas," Sonny said, resting his forehead against Abe's. "Although, I do kind of have something for you." He felt Abe tense. "Don't panic, it's not that kind of something." *Not yet anyway.*

Sonny reached into his coat pocket and brought out a thin, rectangular box, too big for jewelry. "Open it."

Abe took the box and opened it to find a silver-toned key on a keyring. He looked up at Sonny with a smirk. "You made a big deal to give me a key to your house?"

"Well, I mean, it can just be that if you'd like. But I was kind of thinking, maybe when we get back and you've had time to think it over, maybe it could be our house."

Abe looked stunned. "Sonny…"

"Only if you want it to be. If not, then yes, that's your key to my house." Sonny brushed Abe's hair back from his brow.

Abe looked down at the key in his hand, seeming to

consider the choice it represented: his key into Sonny's life, or the key to their life together.

"Think it over. There's no deadline and no pressure." Sonny kissed his temple. "I just wanted to put the offer on the table."

Abe wrapped his fingers around the key and looked up at Sonny. "You and me, huh? Living together? In your house?"

"Our house, if that's what you want."

Abe nodded, holding the key tight. "Our house."

Sonny beamed. "Yeah?"

"Yeah," Abe said.

Sonny picked him up then, kissing him and jarring the empty box from his hands.

But not the key. Never the key.

Acknowledgements

To my mom, Lola Baisden. Not only did you believe in me when self-doubt crept in, but you eagerly answered all of my Texas-related questions. I hope you know that this is not only an ode to my Texas roots, but also a vague homage to you and dad.

To my sister, Victoria Jeffers. I trust your opinions and thoughts on my writing and you never let me down. You're in this for the long haul, I hope you know that.

To one of my best friends, Brittney Hooker. I wasn't as nervous this time around, and you definitely helped with that. Thank you for the encouragement and cookies!

To my editor, Keren Reed, and my proofreader, Judy Zweifel. You're both awesome and this story wouldn't be as sharp and clear without you. I'd like to think I'm growing as a writer, but your work gives me that extra boost of confidence.

To my family, friends, and day-job coworkers not mentioned above, once again, you rock! I thank each and every one of you for your encouragement and interest in my writing. It truly means a lot.

And finally, who would I be if I didn't thank you, reader? I hope that you enjoyed reading *Blind Faith* enough to join me on the next leg of Sonny and Abe's story.

Delphia Baisden is a proud indie author. In 2016, she finally decided to use her passion for writing to tell the love stories of her heart and hasn't stopped since. She is an avid rock 'n' roll fan who feels most comfortable in a band tee and a pair of jeans. She currently lives in a small town near Columbus, Ohio, with her mom, Lola.

For more information, please visit delphiabaisden.com.

Check out her first novel, *Credence*, at mybook.to/Credence.